THE SECRET DRAGON

THE SECRET DRAGON

Ed Clarke

PUFFIN

PUFFIN BOOKS

UK | USA | Canada | Ireland | Australia
India | New Zealand | South Africa

Puffin Books is part of the Penguin Random House group of companies
whose addresses can be found at global.penguinrandomhouse.com.

www.penguin.co.uk
www.puffin.co.uk
www.ladybird.co.uk

First published 2019
001

Text copyright © Ed Clarke, 2019
Chapter head illustrations copyright © Simone Krüger, 2019

The moral right of the author and illustrators has been asserted

Set in 13/20 pt Bembo Book MT Std
Typeset by Jouve (UK), Milton Keynes
Printed and bound in Great Britain by Clays Ltd, Elcograf S.p.A.

A CIP catalogue record for this book is available from the British Library

ISBN: 978-0-241-36051-4

All correspondence to:
Puffin Books
Penguin Random House Children's
80 Strand, London WC2R ORL

For Miriam, Rose and Rachel

Prologue

It was probably a Saturday or a Sunday when it happened, most likely in early September. But those details weren't important to Mari. What was important was she remembered very clearly what had happened that day. It was one of those things that changed you forever, made you somehow special, but not in a way you'd ever wish on yourself.

Mari's parents had taken her for a picnic on the clifftops at Worm's Head in Rhossili, an hour's drive from their farm. When she closed her eyes, she could

still feel the soft bluster of the wind baffling off the great bay; it swept round to an island that snaked out into the sea like a giant plesiosaur trying to break free from the rocky cliffs holding it captive. She could still see her little five-year-old fingers engulfed by one of her father's giant farmer's hands as they picked their way along the path, the roughness of his work-toughened skin scratching reassuringly against hers.

They laid out a blanket beneath a solitary beech tree that had somehow fought off the fierce coastal winds to stand proudly alone. Nestled against its trunk, sipping autumn apple juice her father had pressed himself, Mari had never felt happier.

The storm that blew up behind Worm's Head took them all unawares. Perhaps her parents thought it would pass as quickly as it came. Perhaps they just didn't want to let such a magical day be spoiled by the weather. Whatever the reason, they decided to stay sheltered beneath that brave beech tree.

Except that Mari didn't stay with them. She couldn't remember why she had wanted to run out and play in the rain, but she had. And her father had raced after her and gathered her up in his powerful arms just as a fork of lightning found its way down to him from the darkest cloud in the sky.

Chapter 1

Six years later

Bump, bump, bump.

Mari's head banged repeatedly against the window of the beaten-up Land Rover as it bounced through the uneven field. Mari stared straight ahead, oblivious. This wasn't where she wanted to be.

Bump, bump, bump.

Out of the corner of her eye Mari could see her mum, Rhian, trying to think of something to say.

'Might knock some —'

'Sense into me,' sighed Mari.

Rhian smiled, but Mari didn't turn round. They returned to their customary awkward silence. Rain started spattering the windscreen. Rhian engaged the ancient wipers, and they squeaked and creaked the window a smeary kind of clean.

After what seemed like an age Rhian pulled up in the corner of a field. Mari could see the calf lying on the ground, its breathing rapid and shallow.

Her mum nodded towards it. 'Why don't you go and take a look this time?'

Mari frowned. That wasn't how it usually worked. Normally Rhian would go and see to a sick animal, and Mari would only help if help were required.

'But I don't know what to do.'

'You're old enough now, Mari,' said Rhian with an encouraging nod. 'It would be a help to me.'

But it wasn't that simple. Caring for animals was in Rhian's blood. She had an instinct for it. Mari couldn't even keep a woodlouse in a matchbox overnight without it expiring. Her father hadn't been a natural farmer either – he'd been a geologist – but he did have

green fingers, creating a kitchen garden behind the farmhouse. Everyone said he and Rhian made the perfect team. And then, after the storm, the team was just Rhian and Mari. And it wasn't perfect any more. Now her dad's once beautifully tended garden was a sad, tangled mess, Rhian had to spend all her time in the fields with the cows, and Mari was expected to help. Whether she wanted to or not.

Against her better judgement, Mari creaked open the rusty Land Rover door and rolled out into the rain. It was coming horizontally off the Bristol Channel and made her squint. She bent down in front of the calf, tentatively holding out a hand to pat its head, trying to stay as far away from it as possible.

'What's the problem?' she whispered, trying not to look it directly in the eye.

The calf let out a strangled moo. She could feel it shivering under her hand.

'I know you can't communicate verbally,' she said, 'but I'm going to guess that you're cold, and need some kind of shelter for warmth, so let's get you inside.'

Gripping the calf's flanks, Mari tried to raise it up on to its feet, but it bellowed out in pain.

Rhian was already out of the car and hurrying towards them. 'Mari, stop!' she yelled.

Mari jumped back. 'What?'

Rhian held the calf still. 'It's got a broken leg. You can't move it.'

'But how would I know that?' pleaded Mari.

'I'm sorry, it's my fault,' said Rhian, more quietly now. 'I shouldn't have asked you.'

Chastened, Mari climbed back into the vehicle, and watched through the mud-splattered window as Rhian tended to the calf. She found a bag of Haribo in the glove compartment and guiltily started working her way through it. The bag was finished and discarded on the floor by the time the driver's door opened again.

'I'll need to get the vet out,' said Rhian as she turned the key in the ignition and shifted the gears into reverse.

'Is it OK if I . . . ?' asked Mari, pointing to a sturdy rucksack on the back seat.

'Now?' asked Rhian. 'We've got that fence to repair in the corner paddock. And bales to stack in the barn.'

There was never nothing to do on the farm. And it always needed doing yesterday.

'While it's still light?' begged Mari.

'Do you really have to, love?'

Mari slumped back. She knew her plans were going to have to wait. Just like they always did.

But for once Rhian sighed and relented. 'I suppose the bales can wait till Saturday. But stay away from the cliffs in case there's a rockfall. It's more dangerous when it's been raining, and –'

'Watch the tides. Yes, I know all this, Mum.'

Mari jumped out eagerly before her mum changed her mind. She slammed the door behind her, slung the bag over her shoulder and nodded an apology to the calf.

A spring now back in her step, Mari hiked across the field towards a gate. Climbing over it, she paused for a moment to take in the view. The rain was easing off now and the sun was breaking through the

heavy clouds, throwing shafts of light down on to the Glamorgan coast, across the Channel and on to the Somerset hills beyond. Off to her right, a pristine white lighthouse seemed spot-lit on the clifftop. She smiled to herself and jumped down, making her way along a hedgerow towards the cliff path.

Before long she was down on the beach. She breathed deeply as the sea breeze gently pushed her hair back from her face. This was Mari in *her* element. She swung her rucksack down on to the rocks, pulled it wide open and gazed lovingly inside.

'Hello again, my friends,' she said.

One by one, she lifted out the contents: a large hammer, a chisel, a brush. And, last but not least, a white hard hat and a pair of clear safety glasses.

'Let's get to work.'

Chapter 2

Mari loved this coastline at any time of day, but the 'magic hour' of dusk was her favourite. The sun bathed the limestone cliffs in a warm orange light, and if it was clear enough you could see the great glowing ball drop straight into the narrow patch of sea where it divided Devon from the Pembrokeshire coast. This was when her father used to bring her down to the beach when she was little.

She remembered him telling her stories about the layers of rock and how they were formed, and about

the great sea creatures that had swum in the waters beneath their feet, millions of years ago. At least, Mari had assumed they were just stories – until the day they found a fossil on the beach that proved what he was saying was true.

That fossil was now her most prized possession. It was an Anningella, a scallop shell named after one of the most famous fossil hunters in history, Mary Anning. Her dad had told Mari that when Mary was alive, in the nineteenth century, no one believed her stories either. And not just because giant sea monsters seemed very unlikely, but because she was a woman, and in those days the idea of a woman being a scientist and making important discoveries was seen as ridiculous. And then he had held Mari by the shoulders and said, 'Don't let anyone stop you being who you want to be.'

Mari had never forgotten her father's words and, as she walked along the beach with her fossil-hunting kit, she knew she never would. However much her mum needed her to be someone else, she was going to be the person she wanted to be. She wasn't in the

least bit interested in cows. She was going to be a palaeontologist. A scientist, like her dad. The layered cliffs of the Glamorgan Heritage Coast were like the leaves of a giant history book, just waiting for her to turn the pages. Who knew what ancient creatures might be found between the layers of limestone and shale?

Mari leaped effortlessly from boulder to boulder along the stony beach. She spotted a fresh rockfall just ahead. The cliff where the rock had cleaved away was a bright yellowy orange shining out between the weatherworn strata on either side. The tumbled rocks lay beneath in a great sloping pile. It was like a pirate giant had emptied out her mammoth treasure chest, leaving Mari to hunt out all the jewels. It didn't take long before her eye caught a curving shape cutting across one of the rocks. It was segmented, and looked a little like a snail shell.

Snakestone! Her father would have laughed – because that's what people used to think they were: serpents that had been turned to stone. But Mari knew

better. The fact was far more interesting than the fiction. It was the petrified remains of an ammonite, an extinct sea creature that had lived over 65 million years ago.

Mari patted her hard hat to make sure it was secure, and pushed her protective glasses up the bridge of her nose. Then she knelt down and got to work with her hammer and chisel, chipping away the rock around the ancient animal. The sun was setting gloriously behind her, but Mari wasn't interested in such an everyday occurrence. In the palm of her hand she was holding an ammonite, the first human *ever* to hold it. A jolt of excitement shot through her. She imagined herself rocketing back like a time-travelling explorer to the moment when the creature first fell to the seabed, with ichthyosaurs snapping at prehistoric fish above.

'Nice rock,' said a voice somewhere above her.

Mari jumped up in shock. A boy of about her age was sitting higher up the rockfall, staring down at her. She hadn't seen him before. He had a dark

complexion, a shock of long, fizzing curls, and a fringe that kept blowing into his face.

'Pretty here, isn't it?' he continued, looking out at the sunset.

Mari raised her hand and pointed at the rocks he was perched on. 'You shouldn't be sitting up there,' she said. 'It's dangerous when it's been raining. It erodes the cliffs. Causes rocks to fall.'

'Like these?' He pointed down to the rocks he was sitting on.

She nodded.

'That why . . . ?' He patted his head, indicating her hard hat.

She nodded again.

'What about the . . . ?' He pointed to his eyes with two fingers.

Mari took off her safety glasses self-consciously and folded them up. 'For stray chips,' she said, half under her breath.

The boy smirked. 'Stray chips,' he repeated to himself with a smile.

Mari wasn't sure whether he was teasing her or not. She knew that most people at school thought she was a weird science kid. Ffion in her class refused to sit next to her because she said she was afraid 'Mari might do experiments on her'.

To be fair, Mari had put quite some time into thinking what kind of experiment she would do on Ffion, given the chance, but nothing suitably stomach-churning had yet occurred to her.

'You wouldn't like one in your eye,' said Mari.

'Sounds nasty,' he said, flipping back his fringe. 'Thanks for the tip.'

The boy sounded sincere. Mari wondered if she'd misjudged him. Why was it so hard to work other people out? This was why she was better off without friends. She didn't understand how the being-popular thing worked. It seemed to be based on doing what everyone else did and liking what everyone else liked, and then being nasty about anyone who didn't do or like the same things. But Mari knew what she liked – and she knew it was different from everyone else.

'What are you doing down there anyway?' asked the boy.

Mari decided to cut to the chase. 'I'm a palaeontologist,' she announced.

'Nice,' replied the boy. 'I'm a Methodist.'

Now Mari really didn't know if he was joking.

'It's a scientist who studies fossils.'

'You don't say . . .' The boy smiled as he stood up to leave. 'I prefer animals that still have a heartbeat myself.'

He took a step forward and slipped slightly, setting off a mini-landslide that narrowly missed Mari's feet. He held his hand up in apology. 'Do you have any more of those?' he said, nodding towards her hard hat.

'Not sure I've got any the right size,' said Mari. 'You've got a lot of hair.'

'Well, you're not wrong there,' the boy chuckled, turning to make his way back up the beach. Mari wasn't sure whether he was laughing with her or at her again.

She watched him disappear up over the clifftop before casting her eyes down at the rocks he'd caused

to slide to her feet. One looked different from the rest as it lay there, illuminated by the setting sun – it seemed to have a redder hue. A crack had opened up down the middle, and she knew that all it would take was one blow from her chisel to cleave it in two. Mari couldn't resist. This was the fossil hunter's lucky dip. What would be inside? Ninety-nine times, nothing; one time, something.

The boy was instantly forgotten. She knelt down beside the stone, fitted the end of her chisel into the crack and rested her hammer on it for a moment – partly to prepare for the blow, partly to savour the anticipation. Then she raised the hammer and brought it down on top of the chisel with one swift, accurate crack. The rock fell apart so easily it almost seemed relieved. Mari lifted her safety glasses to get a better look at what had been revealed.

This was not one of the nothingy ninety-nine times. This was most definitely a *something*.

Coiled inside one half of the rock was a tiny, dusty reptilian shape. It couldn't have been more than ten

centimetres long, and looked a bit like a crested newt with an elongated tail, but it certainly wasn't one of those. For a start, it only had two legs at the back, which were more like an eagle's claws than a newt's padded feet. And secondly, and most strikingly, it had two folded-up wings sprouting from its shoulder blades.

Mari's mind ran through the possibilities. An archaeopteryx? A pterodactyl? But it was too small for either of those. It was unlike any fossil she'd ever seen; unlike any animal she'd ever seen, alive or dead.

She cleaned off the dust carefully with her brush, and gently lifted it out of the rock to rest in her palm. It certainly didn't feel as heavy as a normal fossil. She took it down to the sea to wash it, and as she sluiced the last of the dust off its body it gleamed a deep ruby red. She could see all its tiny individual scales shining in the evening light. What was it? Mari was still completely stumped.

She held the fossil up to the day's last light and marvelled at its delicacy. As the sun was sucked beneath the watery horizon, its light seemed to flash a brilliant

green for just a second before disappearing from view. And, as it did so, the tiny creature's tail uncoiled very slowly across Mari's skin, as lightly as the graze of an uncurling fern.

Mari swallowed hard. Whatever this animal was, it certainly wasn't a fossil. This wasn't a creature that was alive 200 million years ago.

It was alive right now.

Chapter 3

Mari had to stop herself trembling. She brought her left hand round to cup her right and hold it still. Every nerve in her body was tingling with the electric excitement of discovery.

The clouds on the horizon were uplit by a blaze of pink and orange, and it cast a warm glow across the creature's crimson body. Mari had already noticed the talons on its two legs, but now that the seawater had washed the dust away she could make out the crest on

its head, which sparkled in the dying light, reflecting back colours like a prism.

The creature languidly swished its tail from side to side, luxuriating in the warm evening air. Mari reached out a shaking hand to stroke it, and the tail coiled itself around her outstretched finger. But it wasn't like a snake squeezing its prey; it was more an expression of affection. So Mari wasn't scared. In any case, she was far too in awe of what she was witnessing to be afraid.

With the animal gently attached to her finger, Mari lifted it to her face for an even closer look. As she gazed on in wonder, the creature slowly unfolded its wings. Backlit by the twilight glow, they were almost translucent, stretching out on each side of its body, as wide as its tail was long. Mari thought she had never seen anything as beautiful before in her life. And then it opened its eyes.

Mari gasped as two bright green pinheads blinked open on either side of the creature's skull, vivid against its ruby skin. Their eyes instantly locked together: earth brown to emerald green.

Suddenly the animal unfurled its tail and fell from Mari's finger on to a large bare rock. Mari yelped, scrabbling to gather it back up. Then she let out another cry, her finger pricked by a sharp talon. Whatever it was, it seemed the beast didn't want to be picked up again. It was dragging itself around on the rock, one wing flapping, the other tucked away at an awkward angle.

'Please don't be broken,' pleaded Mari, glad that her mother hadn't been here to see her drop the delicate creature. 'Please . . . !'

Gently, she tried to scoop it up again, but every time she thought she'd cornered it, it squirmed out of her grasp, whipping its tail to and fro and scurrying under rocks to escape.

'I didn't mean to hurt you,' said Mari, tentatively rolling back stones. 'I'll be more careful, I promise.'

Finally she found it again, cowering in a shadowy nook above a rock pool. Both wings were tucked away now, and it no longer seemed to be hurt. Mari sighed in relief, and peeled off the cardigan she was wearing.

'This is just to keep you safe,' she explained as she threw it over the animal, collecting it up in its makeshift woolly blanket and depositing it in her rucksack. That bag had held plenty of ancient and extraordinary creatures over the years, but this was the first that was in danger of escaping by itself. She pulled the drawstring tight and buckled the straps. With the pink blush of dusk now faded to grey, it was going to get cold and dark very soon. Mari gently swung the bag over her shoulders and set off up the beach for home.

The walk back gave Mari time to think. What would she tell her mum? She ran through the likely consequences in her mind. Firstly, her mother wouldn't trust her to keep the creature alive. Whether or not Rhian was right to think that, the last thing Mari wanted right now was to have it taken away. Secondly, her mother would want to tell someone else about her discovery, and Mari wasn't sure she was ready for that just yet either. Not before she had worked out what it was, at least. Because she knew it was special. She had never heard of a creature that hatched out of stone. It

was likely to be the most important thing she would ever find, and she wanted to know everything she could about it.

By the time she'd reached the back door of the farmhouse, Mari knew she needed to keep the creature a secret. She turned the door handle as quietly as she possibly could, sneaked into the house, and scurried down the hall into the little room her mum used as an office. It was full to the brim with ring binders, piles of papers and books on farming. Mari scanned the shelves, her finger skimming the spines until she found what she was looking for:

Natural History – A Field Guide.

Perfect, she thought. She slipped it off the shelf and tiptoed quietly to the stairs – but evidently not quietly enough.

'Mari?' came her mother's voice from the living room.

Mari's shoulders sagged. She quickly thrust the book behind her back as Rhian appeared at the living-room door, sporting a nervous smile.

'Is this a good time to talk?'

Something was most definitely up, but now was not the time to find out what. All Mari wanted was to get up to her bedroom, but Rhian was still talking.

'So, the vet came out to see the calf this evening.'

In all the excitement, Mari had forgotten about the calf's broken leg. 'Oh. It's OK, isn't it?'

Rhian smiled again and nodded. In her rucksack, Mari felt the mystery creature wriggle. She hoped her mum hadn't noticed.

'It was a new vet,' Rhian went on. 'Just moved to the town. He was really gentle. With the calf, I mean.'

'That's, erm, good,' said Mari. She pointed up the stairs. 'I just need to, you know, go . . .'

Rhian's face fell. 'OK,' she said. 'Fine, you go.'

Mari gratefully rushed past and up the stairs into the bathroom, closing the door firmly behind her. She pulled the rucksack off her back, unfastened it and gently lifted out the cardigan ball. She unpeeled the layers and was relieved to find the creature still in one piece, though she couldn't say the same for her

cardigan. She was wondering how she was going to explain all the talon-picked holes when she heard footsteps coming up the stairs.

'Don't worry, I won't come in,' said her mother from the other side of the door. 'I just wanted to tell you that the vet asked me out to dinner.' Mari tensed up immediately. Her mother had got her full attention now. 'And I said yes.'

'You did *what*?' said Mari, racing to the door and pulling it open a crack.

'He's taking me to The Lighthouse tomorrow night.'

'Tomorrow night?'

'It's been six years, Mari. Maybe it's time.'

'But – but . . .'

Rhian sighed. 'You know, most people wouldn't leave it so long. But when you live in a small town, and you have a child –'

Mari felt a wave of nausea crash over her. She slammed the door shut in a panic, and leaned her head against the door for support.

'Are you OK, *cariad*?' she heard her mother say.

But Mari couldn't reply. The idea of someone somehow stepping into her father's shoes had hit her too hard. It wasn't that her head hadn't expected this moment. It was that her head had been frightened of telling her heart, so it wasn't at all ready. She felt it aching in her chest now.

'I'm sorry, Mari, I know it's not easy,' said Rhian from the other side of the door, more softly now. 'But the past is gone. And if we don't move on, we're no different from those fossils you find on the beach. Just stuck in the same place for eternity.'

Mari could feel a small tear make its way down her cheek.

'It's just dinner, love.' Her mum was almost whispering now.

Mari wiped her cheek with the back of her hand and heard her mother's footsteps slowly receding down the stairs. She rocked gently on her forehead before rolling round and sliding down on to the hard linoleum floor.

The tiny red creature was sitting on top of her cardigan, chewing on a frayed end of wool.

'I prefer the past,' said Mari quietly to the little reptilian thing.

Immediately it stopped chewing and made its way over to where Mari's hand was resting on the floor. Then it unfurled its tail and wound it around her little finger in a tiny embrace.

Chapter 4

Mari sat at her desk. If the beach was her hunting ground, her bedroom was the nest she brought all her treasures back to. Ammonites, brachiopods and trilobites lined the shelves, and fossil pictures messily papered every spare patch of wall. There were meticulous pencil drawings that Mari had sketched herself, a photograph from the *Llanwerydd Post* of Mari showing TV palaeontologist Dr 'Griff' Griffiths from *Dinosaur Hunt* the Anningella she had found with her dad, and, in pride of place on her bedside table, the

Anningella itself. But nowhere was there a picture that remotely resembled the creature now warming its cold blood in the spotlight of her angle-poise lamp, like a lizard on a sun-drenched wall.

Mari leafed through the pages of her mother's natural history book. It showed 5,000 species, all beautifully illustrated. She had worked her way through the entire section on reptiles, but drawn a complete blank. Mari frowned. If this wasn't a living creature that anyone knew of, could it be one that was believed to be extinct? It wouldn't have been the first time that had happened. Back in the 1930s, a woman named Marjorie Courtenay-Latimer had discovered a fish called a coelacanth, which had been thought extinct for 65 *million* years. They called that a 'living fossil'.

Mari reached for her glossy signed copy of *Dr Griff's The Dinosaur Hunter*. It had a picture of him on the front, wearing a leather biker jacket and crouching next to a dusty fossilized skeleton. Inside it was bursting with full-colour diagrams and illustrations of dinosaurs and their remains. She held the book

open next to the winged creature, and whipped through the pages, trying to find a match. The reptile looked on curiously until Mari finally ran out of pages, and let the book fall shut.

'So, if you're not an animal that's alive today,' she said to the quizzical lizard, 'and you're not an animal that's extinct either, what on earth *are* you?'

She wished she could have asked her dad about it. There's no way he wouldn't have known . . .

'Of course!' she said out loud, immediately jumping out of her chair. She pulled open her wardrobe and reached into the darkest recesses at the back. She hauled out a battered cardboard box barely held together with brown packing tape, and spread the contents around on the floor. They were her dad's old geology books and magazines, which she'd managed to stop her mum taking to the charity shop.

First she worked her way through a pile of books – *Principles of Geology*, *The Ancient Changes of the Earth*, *Rock Trails of South Wales*. Nothing there. Mari next

rifled through a pile of his dog-eared *International Journal of Science* magazines. 'The Molecular Tuning of Electroreception in Sharks'? She didn't even know what that meant. 'Dark Days of the Triassic: The Lost World'. Maybe . . . It was about an asteroid that might have wiped out whole species in South Wales 200 million years ago. It talked about lizards that looked like monkeys, and crocodiles that walked upright like dogs. But there was no reference to two-legged reptiles with wings. She slumped to the carpet in despair.

But then she noticed an old hardback book, hidden beneath the magazines. She pushed back the journals and held the book up to the light. At one time it would have been a deep wine colour all over, but decades of exposure to sunlight had faded the spine to pink. A dragon was embossed on the cover.

Mari turned the book over in her hands to read the gold print on the spine: *Folk-Lore and Folk-Stories of Wales* by Marie Trevelyan. This wasn't a book about

natural history, or a scientific magazine; it was a book about legends. What was it even doing in her dad's box? She opened the cover and, in a child's handwriting, saw an inscription.

Jonathan Jones. September 1990

It *was* her father's book – but from when he was a boy, the same age as Mari was now.

Her finger slid across the chapter headings: 'Water-horses and spirits of the mists', 'Corpse-candles and phantom funerals', 'Weird ladies and their work'.

Mari snorted. It was all ridiculous. Made-up creatures to scare little children. But then her finger came to rest on Chapter XIII 'Dragons, serpents and snakes' and curiosity got the better of her. She flipped to the relevant section, the unmistakable stale scent of old paper wafting up to her nose. And there, on the first page of the chapter, she found it – not a photograph or a painting, but an intricate drawing

of a winged dragon with a long tail and two clawed legs. Underneath was written the caption: *Gwiber, or Wyvern*. Mari hungrily scanned the text that followed.

An aged inhabitant of Penllyne, who died a few years ago, said that in his boyhood the winged serpents were described as very beautiful. They were coiled when in repose, and 'looked as though they were covered with jewels of all sorts. Some of them had crests sparkling with all the colours of the rainbow.'

Mari stopped reading and looked across at the creature. She angled the lamp to shine on its crest. Just as it had on the beach, the crest sparkled with colour. It looked *exactly* like the picture in the book. The creature opened one eye, as if it knew it had been found out.

'*Gwee-ber*,' Mari said quietly to herself with her best Welsh pronunciation. 'You're a gwiber.'

She turned back to the book.

He said it was 'no old story, invented to frighten children', but a real fact. His father and uncles had killed some of them, for they were 'as bad as foxes for poultry'.

The gwiber stretched out its claws, opened its jaws wide and yawned.

'You're not an old story either,' Mari whispered to the serpent, reaching out to let it curl its tail around her finger again. 'You're very real.'

But how could a creature thought fictional actually be fact? How could science not know about it? Questions led to more questions and made her head spin. How had it survived encased in rock? Was it some kind of epic hibernation? How was it possible that this creature was still alive?

Then, slowly, a new realization began to seep into her brain. This animal would cause a sensation. This was no dinosaur skeleton, or even a 'living fossil'. This was a mythical creature. A living, breathing *dragon*

lying beneath the desk lamp in her bedroom on Dimland Cross Farm.

Mari's mind really began to whir now. This wouldn't just make the front page of a science journal, it would hit news headlines around the world. Maybe the reptile would even get named after her, like the Anningella was for Mary Anning. Probably something in Latin like ... *Pterodraco mari*! This was her chance to be a real scientist. To be who she wanted to be.

A lump rose in Mari's throat as she remembered her father's words to her. She instinctively reached out for his name, embossed in biro at the front of the book. She ran her fingertip across it, imagining his eleven-year-old self carefully crafting the letters, tongue pushing against the inside of his cheek in concentration. She wished more than anything that he could be here to share this moment with her.

And that's when she thought of it. An idea so perfect and fitting, it chased away her sadness. She would name this new species after her dad. *Pterodraco*

jonathani. Jonathan's Dragon. That way he would share in this moment with her. They would go down in scientific history together. And, in some way, maybe this little creature might bring a part of him back to life.

But just as her heart warmed to this feeling, worries started creeping into her head. The second she showed the dragon to anyone, it would be taken away and she would never see it again. She knew what had happened to Mary Anning. No one had believed her when she first discovered an ichthyosaur skeleton, because she was a woman. And then, after she convinced them, male scientists had taken all the credit! Mari's heart sank at the thought. She couldn't let that happen to her. It had to be the name *she* had chosen. The name that would commemorate her father and no one else. *Pterodraco jonathani*.

Still, she knew she couldn't do this alone. She needed an adult to help her. And that definitely wasn't her mum. She'd never believe Mari could be trusted to look after a living creature. And, anyway, she was

more interested in this new vet than in remembering Mari's dad. Mari glanced over at her *Dinosaur Hunter* book and pulled it down from her desk. Inside was another inscription – a dedication that read:

Keep digging, Mari! One day I'll be working for you!

Dr Griff x

Yes, Dr Griff would understand. He was a scientist too, after all. And one who worked with young people, listened to their opinions and took them seriously. She would take the dragon to him, and together they would march up the steps of the Natural History Museum in London and tell those experts that everything they thought they knew was wrong! Her dad would be so proud of her . . .

But how would she find Dr Griff? It wasn't going to be easy. Then she looked back at the newspaper cutting of them together. It was at a book signing at her school last year. He must visit schools all the time,

and do talks for the public too. Maybe the fact that he was famous would actually make it easier to track him down . . .

'Stay there, *Pterodraco jonathani*,' she ordered with a finger point. 'Not that you can understand a word I'm saying.'

The dragon looked back up innocently as Mari slipped sideways out of the door before tiptoeing quickly down the stairs.

Fortunately, Rhian was watching *Countryfile* in the living room. For once, Mari was glad. For the next hour her mum would sit there, riveted by tales of poorly pigs, beetroot blight, or the latest advances in llama farming. Still, Mari was as quiet as possible as she slid a dusty old computer bag out of the cupboard by the door before creeping up the stairs two at a time and back through her bedroom door.

Where was the dragon? It was no longer basking under the lamp on her desk. She scanned the room, but it was nowhere to be seen. Her eyes flicked to the window, and her stomach lurched. The top part was

slightly open. How could she have been so stupid? She rushed over and searched the sky for any signs of the missing creature. Nothing.

Then Mari heard a tap, and then another. She looked down at the window sill and saw the dragon behind the curtain. It was hopping and flapping its wings in a vain attempt to fly out through the glass. She breathed out in relief, and slowly pulled the window above her shut. Not that there was any danger of the dragon reaching up that high. Clearly flying was not a skill it had yet mastered. As she watched, it bounced off the windowpane again and fell back on the sill, looking dazed. Mari knocked on the glass with her knuckle to demonstrate that it was completely solid.

'You can't get out that way,' she said. 'Best stay inside where it's warm.'

Delicately, she cupped her hands around the dragon and placed it back beneath her lamp, where it curled up, seemingly contented enough to stay put – for the moment at least. Mari slid a battered old laptop out of

the computer bag. It buzzed and whirred like it had cogs inside instead of circuit boards, before finally sparking unwillingly into life.

Mari googled *dr griff griffiths*. It took forever, but a list of results finally pinged on to the screen. She scrolled down until one in particular caught her eye. She clicked on the link.

It was almost too good to be true. On the screen was a web page advertising a conference on 'Progressive Palaeontology' at a Cardiff hotel. Dr Griff was due to address the conference at 2 p.m. the very next day.

Mari grinned. 'Perfect.'

Mari woke with a start, quickly muffling an instinctive cry as she realized that something was tickling her eyebrow.

Her rude awakening had been caused by the tiny dragon, its tail coiled round her ear, claws hooked into her hair. She could feel its miniature tongue flicking above her eye like a lizard trying to catch flies. She pulled it off her face with a wince as it took a tuft of her hair with it. She placed it on her bedside table and shuffled up into a sitting position.

'We mustn't get distracted,' she said. 'We have an important job to do today.'

The dragon cocked its head on one side as if it were listening.

'Mari!' It was her mother shouting from downstairs. 'Now, please!'

It was another school day, and there was one bus that stopped at the end of the long track to Dimland Cross Farm. There wasn't another for a whole hour, and Rhian certainly wouldn't be taking Mari to school if she missed it. Not when there were animals to feed.

Mari had worked out that if she went to school, got marked as present, and sneaked away at lunchtime, she could catch the train to Cardiff, see Dr Griff before his talk, and be home at the time she would normally be back from school. The problem was what to do with the gwiber. Could she keep it in her school bag the whole morning? After the mess it had made of her cardigan, Mari knew she needed something secure to keep the dragon in.

She leaped out of bed and pulled on her school uniform faster than her mum would ever have thought possible, repeated her slipping-out-of-the-door manoeuvre, and ran downstairs. The radio was on in the kitchen, the kettle was boiling, and Rhian was making some toast with her back to the door, so Mari had to speak quite loudly to be heard.

'Can I have a container, please?' she asked.

'Can you have a what?' replied Rhian without turning round.

'Can I have some sort of container, please!'

Rhian flicked off the kettle and looked over at Mari. 'Are you all right, love?' she asked.

'Everything's fine,' said Mari, trying to speed things along. 'I just have a school project and I need to take a . . . thing into school. In a container.'

'What kind of a thing?' said Rhian.

'An insect. From the garden,' floundered Mari. 'A big one.'

'Are you sure that's a good idea?'

'What do you mean?'

'Just that,' said Rhian, choosing her words carefully, 'I mean, you're better with fossils, aren't you? Than living things.'

Mari pulled a face. 'Fine, I knew I shouldn't have asked you.'

She pushed past her mum, and started rooting through cupboards by her feet. At the back of one she found an old ice-cream tub that looked roughly the right size. She peeled open the lid. It had one lonely-looking mince pie in it.

'Look,' said Rhian. 'I didn't mean –'

'Insects are different from farm animals, you know,' said Mari without looking up. She thrust the container into the air. 'Can I use this?'

'I think the mince pie is past its best, yes,' said Rhian.

Mari stood up. 'An insect's biology is completely different to a mammal's. You'd know that if you'd gone to university.'

Mari instantly regretted what she'd said. Unlike her dad, Mari's mum had left school at sixteen, and

had always been sensitive about not being the 'clever one' in the family.

'I didn't need to go to college to learn about animals, thank you very much.'

'I know, Mum. You went to the University of . . .'

'Life. Yes I did.'

'Lucky you didn't have to travel too far though,' added Mari under her breath.

'Pardon?' Rhian bristled suspiciously.

'Nothing,' said Mari quickly, heading for the door.

'You'll need to punch some holes in it,' Rhian called after her. 'So it can breathe.'

'I knew that,' said Mari. 'That's basic science.'

'And maybe some water,' added Rhian.

'OK!'

Mari stomped back upstairs. There was no way she was going to the University of Life if it meant never leaving Llanwerydd. She threw open her bedroom door, only to find that the gwiber had disappeared.

Again. She looked behind the curtain, but it wasn't there. She regretted not keeping her bedroom tidier. There were a hundred hiding places for a small reptilian creature beneath discarded clothes and scrunched-up pieces of paper.

Mari yanked the duvet off the bed, giving it a good shake, but the only thing that fell out was a careworn teddy that no one was supposed to know she still kept in her bed at night. There was nothing beneath her pillow or under her bed. She threw socks, knickers and shirts into the laundry basket in the corner of the room, but no dragons were revealed.

'Your toast is getting cold!' came a shout from the kitchen.

Mari looked to the heavens in exasperation, and finally her eyes fell on the gwiber, hanging on to the top of her bedroom curtain like a kitten that had climbed a tree without knowing how to get down. It was too high for Mari to reach without standing on something, so she put a chair next to the window and clambered up, but it was still out of her grasp.

'Did you fly up there, little reptile?' Mari said, stretching out her hand and trying to sound as soothing as she could.

The dragon seemed distinctly unsoothed. It scrabbled further up the curtain, ripping the material as it went.

'Come down now, please!' Rhian shouted from downstairs, echoing Mari's own thoughts perfectly. Mari wanted to shout back a response, but she was afraid of scaring the dragon any further.

'Come to Mari,' she cajoled, balancing one foot precariously on her bedside table to edge a little higher. She strained her arms as far as they would go, but the gwiber was still out of reach and the chair was starting to tip.

'It would make things *so* much easier if you were a fossil,' Mari muttered as she heard her mother's footsteps on the stairs. '*Please,*' she implored.

The chair wobbled again, and Mari started to lose her balance just as the dragon leaped off the curtain and plummeted towards the bed.

Jumping off the chair as it fell to the floor with a clatter, Mari snatched the falling creature out of the air and stuffed it into her pocket.

'What on earth is going on in there?' Rhian asked, opening the door just as Mari sat down on her bed looking as innocent as she could manage.

'Sorry, Mum,' she said. 'Did you call?'

'The bus will be here any minute,' said Rhian, looking around the room suspiciously. 'You'll have to eat your toast as you go. Come *on*, Mari!'

And with that she turned on her heel and was gone.

Mari reached into the pocket of her school cardigan and pulled out the gwiber. It looked up to meet her gaze, and if she hadn't been a serious scientist who knew better than to believe animals felt human emotions, she might almost have sworn that it was laughing at her.

She narrowed her eyes disapprovingly. 'It's going to be like that then, is it?' she said.

The tiny dragon nestled contentedly into her palm.

Clearly, it was.

Chapter 6

The schoolyard of Llanwerydd Primary was perhaps the one place Mari liked even less than the farmyard. It wasn't that she minded if no one wanted to sit next to her. It wasn't even that Ffion thought it was funny to pretend she was being electrocuted every time Mari brushed past her. It was more that no one seemed to care about anything that really mattered, yet they all seemed to care about everything that didn't. So Mari didn't think there was much point in trying to fit in.

Today, however, Mari had a secret that would keep her company all day. She strode confidently into the playground, safe in the knowledge that the second half of the day would more than make up for anything bad the first half could throw at her.

Her daydream was interrupted by the sound of a slamming car door and a stifled argument. It was the boy from the beach. His dad was dropping him off in a bright yellow estate, and seemed insistent on kissing him goodbye.

'Have a good day, Dylan!'

Dylan was obviously too mortified to respond. Fortunately for him, though, Mari was the sole witness to the scene.

She took her usual seat, next to no one, and began happily doodling a fossil on the cover of her workbook.

'Nice bug. Is someone sitting here?'

Inevitably, it was Dylan.

'It's a trilobite,' replied Mari. 'And no, it's not a seat that someone sits in.'

He looked confused. 'You mean it's broken?'

'No – it's just not a seat people seem to like,' Mari clarified. 'But *I* like that it's empty.'

'Does that mean I can or I can't?'

'Suit yourself,' she replied.

Dylan looked around the class, but there were no other free places. He lowered himself down gingerly, like he half expected the chair to give way beneath him.

'I'm pretty sure it's safe,' said Mari as he settled in. 'Though I've never tested it.'

She glanced up to see Ffion and her friends casually turning round to look the new boy up and down.

'Hi there,' Ffion said to him. 'I wouldn't sit too close to her,' she continued, nodding at Mari. 'Could be dangerous. You know what happened to her dad?'

Ffion opened her eyes wide, and started to shake as if she'd stuck her finger in an electric socket. Her cronies all laughed as they turned back, but Mari was unmoved. She'd seen this routine before.

Dylan threw her a puzzled look.

Mari sighed. 'My dad died when he got struck by lightning. And Ffion thinks she's being *so* clever.'

'I'm sorry to hear –' he began.

'But then she's also the only vegan who believes pork sausages are meat-free because that's what her dad told her.'

'I heard that, Mari Jones,' said Ffion. 'He *is* the butcher and he would know.'

Mari raised an eyebrow at Dylan before Mr Pugh, their form teacher, broke in.

'Listen up, everyone! I'd like you to say hello to Dylan Moss, who's just moved here from Cardiff.'

'Hel-lo, Dy-lan,' droned the class.

Dylan offered a sheepish wave in return.

'I'm sure Year Six will make you feel very welcome,' concluded Mr Pugh.

'Oh, you can be sure they will,' murmured Mari under her breath.

Dylan turned to her for a second, but Mari wasn't about to elaborate. So instead he took out a pair of reading glasses and started to put them on.

'For the stray chips,' he said, turning back to face the front and pushing the spectacles up the bridge of his nose.

Mari wasn't sure if he was teasing her again, but it didn't matter. She had more important things on her mind.

When the bell rang for lunch, it was an even more blessed relief than usual. Mari raced out of the school gates and ran full pelt for the train station. The 12:56 to Cardiff was just about to close its doors as she arrived, and she jumped through the gap and straight into a seat.

Mari put her bag on her lap and hurriedly unzipped it. She hadn't been able to check on the dragon all morning for fear of someone seeing her. She quickly glanced around the carriage to make sure no one was watching before carefully lifting out the ice-cream container and peeling back the lid.

The little dragon looked up at her a little drowsily, and stretched out a wing. Mari checked the little bit of

sponge she had soaked with water for it to drink. It was untouched, as were the leaves she had put in there too, in case it got hungry. Mari eyed the tiny creature nervously. Had she given it the things it needed? Was it getting enough air?

To be on the safe side, she grabbed a pen from her pencil case, stuck down the lid of the box again, and began stabbing at the top to make some more holes.

That's better, she thought, unpeeling the lid to check if the dragon seemed any perkier. Instead, it was cowering in fear in the corner of the box.

'I'm so sorry!' she hissed, suddenly realizing how scared it must have been watching a giant spike breaking repeatedly through its roof. Mari sighed. She wasn't a natural at this at all. To make matters worse, she realized that a woman sitting slightly further down the carriage had been watching her. When Mari turned round, she hastily buried her face in her book, but Mari couldn't help wondering if she had caught a glimpse of the dragon. The sooner she got to Dr Griff, the better.

Thirty nervous minutes later, the train was pulling into Cardiff Central station. The doors weren't even properly open before Mari was out. It was twenty to two, and somehow she had to get to the hotel where the conference was taking place, find the room where Dr Griff was making his speech, and share the discovery of a lifetime with him before he started at two o'clock. She skidded out of the station on to the streets of Cardiff, having asked a gruff ticket inspector for directions. The city was bursting with people, and she had to dodge and weave to get past them all.

Mari finally found the hotel. It was an enormous, modern high-rise building that loomed over her like an angry teacher, just waiting for her to get something wrong. She felt a sudden anxiety that this was a really stupid idea. But she took a deep breath, pushed her worries aside and pressed on.

Inside, the hotel was even more imposing than its exterior had suggested. A smartly dressed young man stood behind a white wood desk in the middle of the lobby, gazing into a silver laptop like it was a crystal

ball. Mari coughed, trying to get his attention. He didn't look up.

'I'm looking for the Progressive Palaeontology Conference,' she said, in as deep and confident a voice as she could muster.

The man still didn't look up. He just pointed up the grand staircase at the end of the hall, while tapping on the keyboard with his other hand. 'Staircase. Turn right. Lift to the eighth floor. Rhossili Suite.'

Mari waited for a second, just in case he was going to say anything else, but he wasn't. She ran across the lobby and took the stairs two at a time. She slid to a halt by the lifts and hammered the button to call one down.

'Come on, come on,' she urged under her breath, whacking the button again for good measure. She looked at her watch. It was 13:55. It wasn't looking good.

'Going up?' came a voice from her left.

Mari looked round to see a smiling young woman holding open the doors to a lift she hadn't noticed.

She was wearing a black sleeveless T-shirt with a picture of two dinosaur skeletons playing the guitar, underneath which it said MONSTERS OF ROCK. Mari gratefully leaped into the lift and hit the button for the eighth floor.

'You here for Griff?' asked the woman.

Mari nodded.

'You might be waiting a while.'

'What do you mean?' asked Mari as the lift pinged open at the eighth floor to reveal a sea of people. Her heart sank. They were all queuing to get into the Rhossili Suite, half of them carrying *Dinosaur Hunter* books. She slumped back against the wall in defeat. What was she even doing here?

The woman from the lift turned to her with a smile. 'Doesn't mean you shouldn't try.'

Mari nodded her thanks and pushed her way past the throng to the front of the queue, where another woman with a clipboard was guarding the entrance to the suite, crossing people's names off as they came in. She was wearing a name badge that said SANDRA. She

smiled down at Mari – not because she meant it, but because that was part of the job.

'Can I help yourself at all?' she asked, her fixed grin hardly moving.

'Yes,' replied Mari. 'I have something very important to show Dr Griff.'

'Do you have a ticket for the talk?'

'I'm sorry, no, I don't.'

'Well, if yourself would be so kind, I'm afraid I have to look after the people that do,' said Sandra, turning away from Mari and back to the queue.

'But it's *really* important,' said Mari. 'Like, *incredibly* important.'

Sandra ignored her completely, continuing to tick people off her list. Mari tugged at the woman's clipboard to get her attention. This did not go down well.

'Dr Griffiths is on a very tight schedule and today is not a *school* visit. So if yourself would be *so* kind . . .' Sandra wrestled her clipboard back.

'But I have to tell him about something that will CHANGE HISTORY,' insisted Mari desperately,

ripping the ice-cream container out of her bag, peeling back the lid and brandishing it dramatically at the woman like she was letting loose all the demons of hell.

Despite herself, Sandra couldn't help but peer into the box. Mari waited for her expression to change from anger to sheer amazement, but instead her lips pursed in disgust.

'You want to show him a dead newt?'

'What?'

Mari turned the box round to face her. The gwiber lay on its side, eyes closed, its wings tucked tightly into its body, and it wasn't moving.

At all.

Chapter 7

'No!' urged Mari. She shook the box to try and wake up the dragon, but it just slid lifelessly from one side to the other. 'Wake up!' she pleaded, rubbing the reptile's back in an attempt to massage some life back into it.

'You must move yourself aside now,' said Sandra. 'You're blocking a fire exit.'

Mari started to panic. 'But Dr Griff can help me. I *need* him to help me. I'm no good with living things!'

Sandra looked down at her. 'Lucky for you then,' she said. 'That animal is most definitely dead.'

Mari stared forlornly down at the little creature huddled in the corner of the box. The dragon couldn't be dead. It just *couldn't* be.

'Hey there,' came a different voice.

Mari looked up. It was Dr Griff! He was wearing a headset with a microphone attached to it, and the young woman in the MONSTERS OF ROCK T-shirt was standing next to him, smiling. 'Nita here said you were looking for me. Made me come all the way out when I was just about to start, you know.'

For an instant Mari froze, then she whipped the box behind her back to hide it. There was no way she was going to tell Dr Griff how she'd just killed the most important discovery in all of natural history.

'I'm sorry, I don't have all that long,' said Dr Griff. 'What can I do for you?'

Mari laughed nervously. She had no idea what to say. Another awkward moment passed between them all.

'Well,' said Dr Griff, finally breaking the silence. 'It's been *really* fun to meet you, but, you know, the Cenozoic Era is coming to an end and –'

Nita nudged Griff, a little harder than was necessary. 'Ha! That was a little geology joke there. I tell you what . . .' He pulled a business card out of his pocket. 'In case you remember what you came to see me about . . .'

And with that he turned and disappeared back into the auditorium.

Nita gave Mari a sympathetic smile. 'You wouldn't be the first to freeze up like a fossil in front of him. Don't be afraid to email though, OK?'

Mari watched Nita follow Griff into the hall, stuck his card in her pocket and dropped her head in defeat. She had come all the way here only to mess everything up.

Suddenly Mari felt the box behind her back twitch. As if a tiny body had moved . . . She whipped it round, praying she hadn't imagined it.

'I know you don't understand me, *Pterodraco jonathani*,' she whispered, 'but . . . *please* be alive.'

As if in answer, the gwiber let out an almost imperceptible breath.

'Thank you! Thank you!' said Mari, desperately trying to work out what to do.

She looked down at the untouched sponge. Was the dragon just dehydrated?

Mari squeezed the sponge gently so that the liquid within kissed the dragon's lips, but the gwiber turned its head away with such distaste, she might as well have been trying to feed it acid. She tried once more, but the dragon just turned its head the other way before letting it flop down again.

Mari stared at the limp creature, completely frozen with fear. 'Don't die now,' she begged. 'I'm talking to you, and I'm telling you: please don't die.'

She looked around for any kind of help, but none was at hand. The hallway was empty apart from a table laid out for tea and coffee. She hurried over. Was there anything here that might help? Tea bags, little pots of milk, small sachets of sugar . . .

Wait – baby animals drank milk, didn't they? And this was a newly hatched dragon. It was worth a try. Mari plucked a pot from the basket and ripped off the foil lid. She gently held it to the dragon's lips.

'Come on,' she urged. 'Try this.'

Finally, eyes still closed, the dragon's tiny tongue flashed out to taste the milk. And then again. Slowly its eyes opened and its head began to turn, until it was lapping like a kitten.

Mari blew out a breath in relief. She reached out to stroke the animal's scaly head. It was so small, so vulnerable, and so dependent on her.

The gwiber, however, was more concerned with drinking. It made short work of the milk in the pot, so Mari grabbed hold of another. But no sooner had she opened it than the dragon had finished it. She picked up another, marvelling at how something with such a tiny body could absorb all that liquid. Just how long had it been entombed in that stone? A hundred years? More? Mari was trying to calculate how many

dinners it might have lost in its incredible hibernation when it suddenly stopped drinking, as if it had been filled right to the top and couldn't hold even one drop more.

It stretched out its neck, opened its jaws as wide as they would go, and let out a wheezy belch. Mari's nose twitched, and she shrank back in disgust – the tiny dragon's breath smelled of thousand-year-old eggs.

'Well, I guess you're OK now,' she said. 'Come on. We need to get home.'

Chapter 8

Mari carefully replaced the lid on the ice-cream
container, sealing the dragon back inside, and slipped
it into her bag. A clock on the wall nearby read 14:20.
If she was going to get home without arousing her
mum's suspicions, she would have to run for the train
back.

She took off down the hall, bag swinging, feet
pounding. In the lift, she thought she could hear some
tiny knocking sounds coming from her bag, but she
didn't have time to investigate. She was out of the lift,

past the well-dressed man, who still didn't look up from his laptop but droned, 'Do come again,' as Mari whisked out through the revolving door and on to the street.

As she approached the station, though, she realized that something was poking her in the back.

'Ow!' she cried as she put her return ticket through the barrier.

A man wearing a fluorescent jacket gave her an odd sideways glance. 'What's in the bag, miss?' he asked suspiciously.

She grimaced back at him. 'Just my homework.'

'Your homework normally bounce around, does it?' asked the man, coming over to see what was what.

Mari took the bag off her shoulders. Something was clearly thumping against the sides, making it jerk left and right. And though she knew that this something was a tiny dragon which must have escaped from its temporary home, she had no intention of letting the station official find out.

'Oh, that?' she said. 'It's a . . . science experiment. It's quite . . . volatile.'

'I'm not sure if you should be taking it on public transport, in that case,' he said, backing off a little.

'It's perfectly safe,' Mari replied, before adding in her most serious voice, 'in the right hands.'

The man didn't look happy, but before he could say anything else, an irritated old lady starting rapping him with the handle of her walking stick.

'Young man,' she said, 'this gobbly machine has swallowed my ticket!'

Mari took her chance and ran off down the corridor to her platform. It wasn't until she'd found the most tucked-away seat on the train that she dared investigate further. Her bag was still jerking from side to side as she put it down on the window seat.

'Calm down,' she hissed, looking around to make sure no one else could hear. It was fortunate that there were only a couple of other people in the carriage, as the gwiber wouldn't stop thwacking to and fro, and the bag was shuffling itself off the edge of the seat. Mari only just managed to catch it before it dropped on to the floor.

'OK, OK,' she growled. 'What's the matter?'

She knew she had to open the bag to find out what was going on. Very cautiously she pulled down the two zips at the top until there was a gap big enough to see inside. She peered in to see the dragon crouched at the bottom. It looked up at her, its big green eyes radiating innocence.

'Will you make up your mind?' she said sternly. 'One minute you're half dead and the next you're thrashing around like a sheepdog with an itch.' The dragon swished its tail from side to side like a cat getting ready to pounce. 'This is one science experiment that needs to go back in its box.'

She reached in and grabbed the container with one hand, swirling her other hand round to try and catch hold of the gwiber. It wasn't as easy as she'd hoped. It ducked and weaved and slipped between her fingers, refusing to be captured.

'That milk's given you a little too much oomph,' said Mari, both hands now engaged in a vigorous

dance with the reptile inside the backpack. 'I'm just glad you can't use those wings properly yet.'

'Tickets from Cardiff!'

'Really?' muttered Mari, flustered. 'Now?'

A ticket inspector was making his way down the aisle. Mari let go of the container and tried to pull her ticket out of her pocket with one hand, while the other kept wrestling with the dragon.

'Here you are,' she said, brandishing her ticket at the inspector with the best smile she could muster.

'You're a bit young to be out without your parents, aren't you?' came the reply.

'Dad's dead,' said Mari abruptly, employing her favourite tactic for shutting down a conversation.

'Oh,' said the inspector, punching her ticket. 'I'm sorry to hear that.'

As he turned to leave, Mari felt the dragon suddenly shoot up her arm and out of the bag. She spun round to see it perched on the luggage rack above her head.

'Oh, so *now* you can fly,' she said, quickly checking that the inspector hadn't seen.

He was halfway down the carriage now, his back to Mari, speaking to a surly-looking teenage boy who was refusing to take off his headphones.

'Come back down this minute,' she hissed, reaching up to grab the dragon. But it seemed to have no desire to go back into the dark backpack. It sprang from the rack above her and opened its wings to sail on to the one on the opposite side of the carriage. She dived towards it, but it flew straight back the other way. As soon as Mari made a move, it immediately went in the opposite direction, seeming to enjoy the new game.

'Oh, come *on.*'

Mari desperately looked up and down the carriage to make sure that they were still unobserved. The inspector had moved further along. The surly boy was bashing at a game on his phone.

'OK, you need to come to me now,' she said, beckoning gently with one hand and trying to keep

her temper. 'I bet Mary Anning never had this trouble,' she added under her breath.

Mari moved very slowly towards the gwiber, and for once it didn't fly off. She was almost touching it when –

'You want coffee? You want tea?'

Mari froze, before spinning round and dropping into her seat. A smiling, dreadlocked man pushing a drinks trolley had just appeared through the door from the next carriage.

He smiled at Mari. 'I got nice shortbread biscuits . . .' he offered in a warm Caribbean accent.

Mari fixed a grin on her face and shook her head, praying that he would keep going. Unfortunately he was the talkative type.

'I got them little cans of fizzy cola . . .'

Behind the steward, Mari could see the dragon eyeing something on the trolley. Her eyes opened wide as she spotted a wicker basket full of milk pots sitting next to the flasks of tea and coffee.

'How much for some, er, milk?' asked Mari, pointing at the basket.

'Oh, those you can have for free,' said the man. 'You just help yourself.'

Keeping one eye on the gwiber, Mari grabbed a huge handful and stuffed them into her backpack. 'Thank you.' She nodded to him.

'Thirsty girl,' he half whistled to himself as he moved off.

The dragon arrowed down from its perch, missing the man's departing dreadlocks by centimetres, and diving straight into Mari's backpack. As quickly as she could, she ripped the top off one of the pots and popped it into the ice-cream tub. The dragon followed, and she whipped the lid back on. This time, she kept the box on her lap, holding the top firmly down between her hands.

'You, *Pterodraco jonathani*,' she announced, 'are trouble.'

When Mari finally made it back to the farm, she raced straight up to her bedroom. She checked that the door was firmly closed, as well as the window, before

letting the dragon out of its box. It flopped on to her desk, looking a little dazed. She switched on her desk lamp so that it could bask in the warmth.

'I'm sorry about all the to-ing and fro-ing. It's all part of a plan,' she explained. 'I promise.'

The gwiber looked at Mari out of the corner of one eye as she pulled out Dr Griff's business card.

'Dr Griff will help us, I know he will.'

A knock on her bedroom door made her jump.

'Mari, can I have a quick word?'

It was Rhian.

'Don't come in!' Mari blurted.

In a flash, she had shoved the dragon back into the ice-cream container, thrown open her wardrobe and stuffed it inside before slamming the doors firmly shut. She dashed over to her bedroom door and pulled it wide open.

'What are you up to in there?' asked Rhian.

'N-nothing,' said Mari, not at all convincingly.

Rhian raised an eyebrow, but clearly had other things on her mind. Mari almost didn't recognize her

mum. Gone were the usual muddy jeans and baggy wool jumper, and in their place was a stylish black dress that Mari couldn't remember ever seeing before. Instead of being scrunched into a messy topknot, Rhian's freshly dried hair was softly skimming her shoulders.

In all the day's excitement, Mari had forgotten about her mum's date. She felt her face harden. 'I thought you were just going to The Lighthouse,' she said.

'Is it too much?' Rhian asked anxiously. 'He'll be here any minute.'

As much as Mari hated the idea of her mum going out with a man who wasn't Mari's father, she could tell that she was nervous.

'No,' admitted Mari, reaching out to hold her mum's arm for a second. 'You look . . . nice.'

Her mum seemed to relax at her touch. 'Thanks, love,' she said.

Mari managed a little smile in return.

'Oh,' said Rhian, suddenly remembering something. 'I meant to tell you before: Gareth – he's the vet – is a

single parent too, and he didn't want to leave his son on his own tonight, so I told him to bring him over – you could keep each other company while we're out.'

'Seriously?' Mari couldn't believe her mother had thought this was a good idea. 'I'm babysitting?'

'He's not that young,' replied Rhian. 'Pretty much the same age as you. It might be fun.'

Mari doubted that intensely. Now she was going to have to spend an awkward evening with a boy she didn't know while her mother went out with a man who wasn't Mari's father, all the while trying to hide the fact that there was a dragon in her wardrobe.

'Okayyyy,' she said, not really meaning it.

'Great.' Rhian smiled. 'Thanks, love.'

Outside, they could hear the sound of a car crunching up the track to the farm.

'That must be them,' said Rhian apprehensively. 'Try to be polite, Mari. And please try and talk about something other than fossils. Not everyone likes fossils, *cariad*.'

But before Mari could protest, she caught a glimpse through the window of the vehicle pulling up. Her stomach lurched.

The car outside was a bright yellow estate.

And getting out of the front passenger seat was Dylan.

Chapter 9

'We could watch some TV?' said Mari finally, after a silence that felt like it had lasted since the Cretaceous period.

She and Dylan had squeezed themselves into opposite ends of their inconveniently small sofa.

'Don't think there's anything on,' he said.

If Mari had felt embarrassed in her hard hat when she first met Dylan on the beach, this evening was a whole lot worse. Too many of her secrets were already exposed.

'Is it long since, you know, your dad . . . ?' Dylan's question tailed off.

'Not really long enough for my mum to be dating,' replied Mari.

Another awkward silence. Mari considered asking about Dylan's mum, but didn't know how to.

'Can I use your bathroom?' he asked at last.

'Upstairs on the right,' replied Mari, glad to have something to say.

Dylan rocked himself off the sofa and made his way out of the room. Mari's relief was short-lived as she remembered what other secret she was keeping upstairs.

'Do you want a drink of something?' she shouted up the stairs, trying to sound calm.

'Sure, thanks,' came the reply.

Mari knew that it would look odd to follow him up, so she busied herself by hunting around in the kitchen for something decent enough to offer a guest. She relaxed when she heard the toilet flush, but started to

get nervous again when the sound wasn't followed by footsteps coming down. She shovelled some ice into a glass of supermarket cola, hoping that Dylan wouldn't notice the difference, and hurried upstairs.

'You shouldn't be in here,' she snapped as she rounded the corner into her bedroom.

'Sorry, the door was open,' said Dylan. 'I saw the pictures on the walls. They're good.'

Mari calmed down a little when she saw that he was only looking at her fossil sketches. 'Thanks,' she said. 'Mum says other people don't like fossils.'

'Not true,' said Dylan, examining a drawing of an ammonite more closely. 'I just wish the creatures were still alive.'

Mari laughed nervously.

'So this is what you were doing on the beach . . .'

She nodded. 'Finding, not drawing.'

Dylan opened his mouth to say something else but, before he could, from the wardrobe came an unmistakable scratching sound.

'I brought you this,' Mari said loudly, thrusting the cola into his hands.

The scratching turned into thudding. Mari wished she had put something heavy on top of the ice-cream tub to keep the lid on.

'Can you hear that?' said Dylan, taking the drink.

'You hear all kinds of creaks in old houses.' Mari smiled innocently. 'Would you like a slice of lemon with that?'

'No. Thanks. There's definitely something in your wardrobe, though,' Dylan insisted. He started towards it.

'It's probably my hamster,' Mari said quickly.

'You keep a hamster in the wardrobe?'

'It's . . . nocturnal,' she said, as if that explained everything. She slid round him to bar the way. 'And it doesn't like people.'

Dylan narrowed his eyes. Then he smiled. 'You're a terrible liar. What's *really* in there?'

'I didn't like to say,' she said defensively. 'I don't want to freak you out.'

'My dad's a vet. I've seen all kinds of weird pets.'

Mari looked him squarely in the eye, weighing up her next move carefully. 'It's rats,' she blurted. 'We've got rats.'

Dylan took a step back, grimacing slightly. 'Oh.'

Mari warmed to her theme, pleased to have finally found something that seemed to put him off. 'It's a bit embarrassing, but they get everywhere. If we don't keep the doors firmly closed.' She grabbed a large fossil off a shelf and leaned it up against the wardrobe. 'There, just to be sure.' She laughed nervously and pulled Dylan out of the room. 'You won't hear them downstairs.'

Dylan cast a concerned glance behind him as he was dragged back down to the sofa. 'How do you sleep?' he asked. 'With those things . . . scratching.'

'Mum's put some pretty strong poison down,' replied Mari breezily, 'so they won't scratch for long.'

Dylan's face contorted again. Mari found she was beginning to enjoy wielding the power her lie had bestowed on her.

'Crisps?' she asked cheerfully.

Dylan nodded, and took a gulp of his cola. Mari smiled and set off for the kitchen. But just as she snatched up the last packet of own-brand ready salted from the darkest recesses of a cupboard, she heard the unmistakable sound of feet running up the stairs.

'Dylan!' she yelled as she raced out of the kitchen.

'I just need to see for myself!'

Mari leaped up the stairs two at a time, and burst through the door into her bedroom. But she was too late. The wardrobe doors were wide open, and Dylan was staring into it, open-mouthed.

'That's not a rat,' he said.

Chapter 10

'This absolutely, positively, has to remain a secret,' said Mari.

Dylan wasn't listening. He couldn't tear his eyes away from the tiny creature cowering in the corner of its box, caught in the sudden glare of attention.

'It's . . . it's a dragon.'

'Technically,' said Mari, 'it's a gwiber.'

'A gweeby?'

'Gwee-*ber*,' corrected Mari. 'It's Welsh for wyvern. A two-legged winged dragon.'

'It can't be real . . .'

Dylan reached out to touch it, but the gwiber flapped its wings and flew up to perch on an empty hanger, making it swing back and forth.

'Does that look real enough?' Mari asked as Dylan's eyes widened in awe.

'Can I hold it?' he asked.

Mari shook her head. 'I don't think it'll let you.'

'Does it have a name?'

'*Pterodraco jonathani.*'

'Terry what now?'

'It's the Latin name I've given it. Jonathan's Dragon. After my dad.'

'I see.'

Mari braced herself for another question about him, but Dylan seemed to think better of it.

'It's a bit . . . formal, isn't it?' he continued. 'Maybe he needs some kind of pet name.'

'I don't see why,' replied Mari stiffly. 'It's not a pet. It's a major scientific discovery. Nor, for that matter, do we know it's a "he".'

'Well, he looks like a "he" to me. And I think the gwiber needs a proper name,' said Dylan. 'In fact, why not "Gweeb"?'

At that very moment the dragon leaped off its perch, swooped out of the wardrobe and landed on Dylan's shoulder. Dylan gasped, then chuckled. 'Well, there you go. That's settled then!'

Mari rolled her eyes. 'He probably just thinks you've got food,' she said, exasperated. 'He's not recognizing his name like some sort of puppy.'

'I think you underestimate him,' said Dylan. 'And you just called him "he". Twice.'

Mari let out a sigh of frustration. 'Fine,' she said impatiently. 'We can call him a "he". For now. Until we know for sure. But "Gweeb"? Really? It sounds like a cartoon alien.'

'I think it's a perfectly good name for a tiny dragon who lives in a wardrobe. Don't you, Gweeb?'

Gweeb nestled into Dylan's neck, which made Mari feel oddly jealous.

'I think I need him back now,' she said, reaching out a hand.

'You're not putting him back in that plastic box, are you?'

'Why not? What would you do with him?'

Dylan laughed. 'Well, you need help from a grown-up, obviously. You've found the world's first ever real live dragon – we've got to tell someone!'

'I'm going to,' said Mari. 'Dr Griff Griffiths. I've got his email address.'

'The Dinosaur Hunter off the telly? What's he going to do?'

'We'll take the dragon to the Natural History Museum together. So I can make sure they name him after my dad.'

Dylan nearly spat out his cola. 'Who do you think you are? David Attenborough? You're eleven years old! Just tell your mum and we'll all be on breakfast TV tomorrow. It'll be *amazing*.'

'I'm twelve in September. And you don't understand, Dylan. If we don't tell the *right* person,

they will *take him away*. It'll be, *Thanks very much, little girl, we'll do all the important stuff from here. You've had your fun, now run along home.* This is the chance of a lifetime, Dylan. For me to change my life. To be the person I want to be.'

'What do you mean?' Dylan frowned. 'What's wrong with your life anyway?'

'It's my chance to be a proper scientist,' Mari explained. 'To say, *Here is my discovery: the* Pterodraco jonathani.'

'So, let me get this straight,' replied Dylan. 'Your plan is to send Dr Griff an email and say, *Hello, I'm Mari, I'm eleven and three quarters and I've discovered a dragon I can fit in my pocket*? You think his first thought is going to be, *Yes, I can trust her scientific opinion. I'd better get right over there to check it out*?'

Now Dylan was saying it out loud, even Mari realized that her plan was not brilliantly thought through. Particularly as she'd not made the best impression on Dr Griff that afternoon. What would Dad do in this situation? Her eyes fell on one of his

scientific journals, and a plan began to form in her brain.

'I'm not going to tell him how old I am,' she announced suddenly. 'I'm going to make a proper scientific study of Gweeb and send my findings for Dr Griff to verify. I'll say I'm Dr Mari Jones from the University of Such and Such, and then he'll have to take it seriously.'

Even though it was entirely off the cuff, Mari was quite pleased with her new scheme.

'What kind of scientific study?' asked Dylan.

'One like Mary Anning would have made,' she told him. 'Drawings, observations, hypotheses. Her work won over the scientific community, even though she was a woman in a man's world. I'll do the same, but as a kid in a grown-up world.'

Dylan nodded slowly. 'OK.'

'OK? What do you mean, "OK"?'

'OK, I'll help you.'

Mari blinked. 'I wasn't asking for your help.'

'No, but you need it.'

'No, I don't. Gweeb is my dragon. I'm doing this on my own.'

'Only if I don't tell anyone.'

Mari spluttered with indignation. 'But – but . . .'

'But I can really help you, Mari. You might know everything about fossilized animals, but I know about living ones.'

'I can learn all that stuff,' Mari protested. 'I've got books.'

'That's why you're keeping a cold-blooded animal in an ice-cream tub in a chilly, dark wardrobe, is it?'

'I was in a rush – I . . .'

Dylan raised his eyebrows.

'All right, all right,' Mari conceded. 'You can help. But remember: you don't need this like I need this. You're my assistant, not my partner.'

Dylan shrugged. 'Whatever.'

'So, now what?'

'I thought I was your assistant . . . Shouldn't you be telling me?'

95

Mari threw back her head in exasperation. Why did the only other person in the world who knew her secret have to be so infuriating? 'I would value your advice,' she said through gritted teeth.

'Well,' said Dylan. 'First of all, we have to make sure the animal is fed and watered. What does he eat?'

Mari had to admit that this hadn't even crossed her mind . . . well, she had to admit it to herself at least.

'I . . . I don't know yet,' she stammered. 'He likes milk . . .'

'But he's a reptile, not a mammal,' said Dylan. 'I wouldn't be feeding him that, if I were you.'

Mari gulped. Dylan didn't know the half of it.

'Whatever,' he went on. 'You really can't keep him in a wardrobe. If he's like other reptiles, he'll need a terrarium.'

'A what?'

Dylan reached up very slowly to lift Gweeb down from his shoulder, making sure to hold his wings tight against his body.

'A terrarium. A glass box to put reptiles in, with heat lamps at the top. They're cold-blooded, so they need artificial warmth.' Dylan carefully turned Gweeb over in his hands, fascinated. 'He really is incredible. Part lizard, part bat, part bird.'

Gweeb didn't seem to care for Dylan's inspection though. His emerald-green eyes sparkled as he swiped at Dylan's hand with one of his talons.

'Argh!' Dylan yelled, letting go.

Gweeb hit the carpet with a thud, but before Mari could gather him up he darted into the air and out through the bedroom door.

'Quick!' she cried.

They dashed after him, giving chase down the stairs and into the living room. But Gweeb was nowhere to be seen. Then Mari noticed a curtain blowing slightly in the breeze. There was a small window open in the corner of the room. She closed her eyes in disbelief.

'I *told* you not to let him out,' she said. 'He was doing just fine in the wardrobe.'

Dylan looked chastened. He licked a bead of blood from his finger. 'I didn't realize his claws were so sharp.'

Mari was unimpressed. 'I thought you knew all about animals.'

'I'm hazier on mythical ones,' Dylan shot back.

'Well, we'd better start learning fast,' said Mari, 'if we haven't already lost him.'

Suddenly, from somewhere outside, a cow bellowed in pain.

'Oh no,' said Mari, turning pale.

'What is it?'

'Milk!'

Mari bolted for the back door and pelted out into the night, with Dylan right behind her. They rounded a corner and careered into an open cowshed. Mari flipped a light switch to reveal a cow lying in the hay, its udder beginning to swell unnaturally. Mari knelt down next to it. There was no doubt what the issue was. Gweeb had bitten it.

'Where is he?' asked Mari, looking around.

'Up there.' Dylan was pointing up into the rafters of the barn. Mari followed his finger, but could see nothing but shadows. That is, until a pair of headlights approaching up the track illuminated the ruby-red body of Gweeb, perched high up on a crossbeam. For a dragon, he was looking very sheepish.

Mari turned round to see the bright yellow car crackling up the stony farm track, and glanced at Dylan in dismay.

Their parents were back.

Chapter 11

'Oh no,' said Rhian as she ran over to tend to the cow. 'What happened? What did you do?'

'Nothing! We just heard it and ran out . . .' Mari tailed off, guilt weighing heavily on her.

'I'll get my bag,' said Gareth, rushing to the back of his car.

'Dad'll fix it, Mari,' said Dylan, coming over. He ushered her off to one side, nodding towards the roof of the barn to remind her of the other problem they

had. How were they going to get Gweeb down without their parents noticing there was a dragon in the cowshed?

While Gareth knelt down next to Rhian to examine the cow, Mari stole a glance up at the dragon. He was buzzing from rafter to rafter, obviously full of energy from the milk he had swiped from the injured cow. Every now and then he paused to look down at them like a naughty toddler who knew he'd done something wrong, and thought running away afterwards was part of the game.

Mari wondered if she shouldn't just confess here and now. Surely her mum was going to find out the truth any minute – wouldn't it look better if she didn't try and hide it?

'I think it's an adder bite,' announced Gareth suddenly.

'What?' said everyone else at once.

'There are two little puncture wounds on the udder. Sometimes cows can lie on a snake they don't know is there, and they get bitten.'

Mari saw her mother turn to look at her, the frustration in her eyes turning to apology.

'She doesn't look like she's been badly poisoned,' continued Gareth. 'I'll give her an injection for the swelling and antibiotics for any infection. She should be fine in a few days.'

'Thank you, Gareth,' said Rhian. 'It's very kind of you.'

While Gareth and Rhian were distracted by the cow, Dylan leaned close to Mari and said, 'Worms.'

'Pardon?'

'Worms. Maybe that's what little dragons eat . . .'

Mari followed Dylan's eyes down to the ground, where a worm was poking out of the mud. She quickly bent down to retrieve it. Gareth and Rhian were still busy with the cow, so she waved it in the air in the direction of the dragon.

'*Gweeb!*' she hissed, as loudly as she dared.

In a flash he swooped down from the rafters and on to her hand to feast on the worm. She cupped him between her palms and breathed a deep sigh of relief.

'Bit of excitement at the end of the evening!' replied Gareth with a strange snorting laugh as he closed up his bag. 'Time to go now, Dylan. Say goodbye to Mari.'

'Goodbye, Mari,' said Dylan.

'Bye, Dylan,' she replied loudly. Then, more quietly, she added: 'Tomorrow morning, back here, nine o'clock. That's when the work really starts.'

Dylan nodded as Gareth shouted over from the car: 'Come on, son! Don't be dawdling.'

Rhian turned to Mari as the yellow estate pulled out of the yard. 'You two get on then?' she asked hopefully.

Mari just shrugged. She wasn't going to give anything away.

'Well, if you can be nice to him, I'd really appreciate it,' Rhian continued. 'You know, in case you see him again.'

Mari sighed. She guessed that meant her mum might be seeing Dylan's dad again.

Rhian seemed to sense Mari's discontent. 'I think he's a good man, Mari,' she said. 'A strange sense of humour, perhaps, but a good man.'

Mari didn't want to talk about her mum's date. It made her feel queasy. And it didn't help that Gweeb was trying to escape from between her cupped palms.

'Argh, you monster!' she blurted out as he scratched her with one of his miniature talons.

'Mari! That's a horrible thing to say,' said Rhian, looking hurt.

'I didn't mean you, Mum, honest,' replied Mari.

'Then who *did* you mean?'

'I . . . um . . . I meant . . .' Mari trailed off. There was nothing she could say without giving the game away.

'Right,' said Rhian. 'In that case you can go straight to bed. And those hay bales need stacking first thing tomorrow.'

'But, Mum!'

'No *if*s, no *but*s. We're farmers – we can't just laze around at weekends like everyone else.'

'But I've got stuff to do!'

'Important fossil-finding business, no doubt. Well, they've been stuck in a rock for a few million years, Mari, so another day isn't going to hurt.'

And with that Rhian stomped off back into the house.

Mari opened her scratched hands to see Gweeb looking up at her as if butter wouldn't melt in his dragon's mouth.

'You see all the trouble you're causing, *Pterodraco jonathani*?'

He gave a little sneezing snort.

'Yes, well, I only hope it's worth it.'

Chapter 12

The next day Mari woke bright and early. She turned straight over to check on Gweeb, who was basking quietly beneath the desk lamp she had left on all night.

He saw her looking over and immediately started opening and closing his mouth in a show of hunger.

'Good morning to you too,' said Mari. 'I'll be back in a minute.'

She yawned her way downstairs, hair still skew-whiff. She could hear the sound of the milking

machine from the dairy and knew it would be at least another hour before her mum was back in for breakfast.

Grabbing a rinsed-out yoghurt pot from the recycling, Mari stepped into her wellies by the back door, found a trowel in the forlorn-looking shed, and trudged over to what used to be her dad's beloved kitchen garden. In one corner sat a compost heap that had long since sprouted weeds, but that Mari knew would provide the richest soil. She dug in with the trowel, and soon exposed a writhing mass of worms. Grimacing, she plucked out three wiggling invertebrates and popped them into the plastic pot.

Back in the house, she plucked one of the tiny milk pots she'd saved from the train out of her school bag, and creaked back up the stairs with Gweeb's breakfast.

'Just one pot this morning, Gweeb,' she told him, peeling back the top of the milk pot. 'We need less craziness and more seriousness. We have science to do today.'

Gweeb looked up from his mini-feast and let out a burp in Mari's direction. Mari wrinkled her nose at the unpleasant smell.

'You're welcome,' she said.

Mari went over to her shelves and slid out a brand-new ring binder, cracked open the cellophane on a set of ten dividers, and filled the folder with A4 paper.

'Now, are we going to stack hay bales this morning?' she asked the dragon, gathering up a selection of highlighters and rolling them into a dinosaur pencil case. 'Or are we going to make history?'

There was a rattling at her bedroom window: the sound of tiny stones being thrown to get Mari's attention.

'Good, he's early,' she said.

She raced down the stairs and threw open the back door.

'I liberated this from Dad's supplies,' said Dylan, holding up a large, clear plastic animal carrier with ventilation slots at the top. 'It's not really big enough

for a flying reptile, but it's warmer than an ice-cream tub, and a lot more secure.'

'Perfect,' said Mari. 'Let's get started.'

They carried Gweeb out to the part of the farm that was furthest from the dairy and the temptations of milk. It was an exposed field with only a few small trees dotting the hedgerows, bent over into contorted curves by the harsh prevailing winds. Off in the distance, the lighthouse twinkled, and beyond that lay the cold, grey Bristol Channel.

Dylan shivered. 'So, what's the plan, Dr Jones?'

'I'll do some tests, you take notes,' said Mari, thrusting her ring binder and a pen into his hands.

Dylan didn't look impressed. 'Couldn't we have done this somewhere warmer?'

'Welcome to the country, Townie,' said Mari. 'We need to observe the dragon's flying abilities and we can't do that near cows. May I begin?'

Dylan rolled his eyes and lifted his pen.

Mari carefully opened the lid of the travel terrarium, and Gweeb looked up at them as quizzically

as a dragon could. She pulled a large ball of string out of her bag and started looping it around his neck.

'Hang on,' said Dylan. 'What are you doing?'

'I'm making a leash,' replied Mari.

'What on earth for?'

'So he doesn't fly away, of course. That would be the end of everything.'

Dylan shook his head firmly. 'But he's a wild animal, not a kite. You might strangle him. We have to train him to come to food, like they do with birds of prey.'

'You think we can train him?'

'Of course,' replied Dylan.

Mari was unconvinced. 'Just so you know, this is going down as your idea.'

She reached back into her bag and handed him a small plastic box full of worms.

'So what do we do first?' she asked.

'Why don't you try telling him what we're doing?'

Mari snorted. 'Because he's a wild animal? And they don't speak English?'

Dylan shrugged. 'If you say so.'

'Fine. Let's try it your way, Mr Dragon Expert. Now, Gweeb,' she continued in her best scientist's voice. 'Today I shall be making some observations about you, and my assistant over there will be noting them down. I shall then write up an article to be verified by Dr Griff Griffiths and published in the *International Journal of Science*. I hope you will help us by cooperating to the best of your ability, and not attempting to fly away.'

Gweeb looked blankly at them.

'Do you think he got all that?' Mari asked Dylan, one eyebrow raised.

'You know that lizards don't like the cold either, right?' said Dylan. 'Shouldn't we get started?'

Mari nodded. 'First observations,' she announced. 'Physical appearance. Colour is deep red. Reptilian scales all over. Eyes are green.'

'We know all this,' said Dylan.

'I know *we* know, but we have to be thorough for those who don't,' replied Mari. 'This is for publication.'

She found the tape measure in her pocket and stretched it out next to the dragon. With some difficulty she managed to unroll Gweeb's tail along the length of it to get an accurate figure.

'Length: 15.2 centimetres from nose to tail.' She spun the tape measure round and extended Gweeb's wings between her fingertips, prompting an eggy hiss from the little dragon. 'Wingspan: 16.5 centimetres. Have you got that?'

'Yes, Dr Jones.'

'You don't have to keep calling me Dr Jones.'

'I think it suits you,' said Dylan with a wry smile.

Mari ignored him and changed the subject. 'Do you have a phone?' she asked.

'Dad won't let me,' said Dylan. 'Why?'

'Because we should take pictures,' said Mari. 'And Mum won't let me have one either.'

'You're pretty good at drawing,' Dylan observed.

'I'm not sure that's enough for the *International Journal of Science*,' replied Mari. 'We'll have to think of something later. Let's keep going.'

Dylan cocked his head to one side and lifted his pen in readiness. 'Yes, Doctor.'

Mari bit her tongue. He wasn't taking this at all seriously.

'Next, texture.' Mari ran her finger along Gweeb's body. 'Soft to the touch. Not slimy.' She prodded the dragon's belly. He squirmed and glared.

'Steady on,' said Dylan.

'This is for science,' said Mari. 'These are important tests.'

'He's still a living thing. You've got to give him a bit of respect.'

Mari was getting a little irritated with Dylan now. 'And you, Dylan, have to respect *science*.'

'Maybe it's better if you do this by yourself,' said Dylan. 'It doesn't seem like you want my help.'

'Well, you may remember that I didn't actually ask for it,' snapped Mari.

Dylan put down the ring binder and held up his hands. 'Fine,' he said. 'I'll leave you to it then, shall I?' He started to walk away.

Mari ground her teeth. He was infuriating, but she was far too worried about what he might do if she let him go. Besides, it would take longer if she had to do all the measuring and all the writing herself.

'OK, wait,' she said finally. 'I would like your help.'

Dylan turned round. 'On one condition,' he said.

'You have conditions now?'

'You let me make sure Gweeb is OK,' he said.

Mari gave him a funny look. 'I don't understand.'

'I mean, make sure he's healthy. And that you don't, you know, hurt him. With your science.'

Dylan sounded just like Rhian. Mari had to gulp down her pride before replying.

'Fine,' she said eventually. 'You can check on the creature's welfare before we carry out any experiments.'

Dylan smiled his approval. 'What's the next test then?' he asked.

'Flying,' replied Mari.

'Fantastic,' said Dylan.

As if on cue, Gweeb sprang into the air, whipping their faces with his tail as he whisked past them. Dylan

followed his trajectory high up into the sky as he swooped and soared at incredible speed. His jaw dropped open in amazement. He turned to look at Mari. She was biting her nails.

'You're sure he's going to come back for the worms?' she asked.

'Relax,' said Dylan. 'And enjoy the show.'

Mari tried not to worry. A small smile crept slowly across her face as Gweeb skirted a hedgerow one minute and then rocketed into the air to chase a sparrow the next.

'Fascinating behaviour,' she said finally. 'Probably hunting.'

'Glad you like it.' Dylan smiled. 'I'll write that down.'

But he wasn't writing yet because, like Mari, he was still staring up into the sky, completely entranced by the dragon's flight. They stood together in silent awe, every now and then looking across at one another to exchange a grin, relishing the moment.

That is until Mari noticed that Gweeb was starting to slow down, his attention caught by something in the distance.

'OK, get the worms ready, Dylan,' she said nervously.

'Why? He seems happy enough –'

Suddenly Gweeb shot off in the direction of the lighthouse on the clifftop a hundred metres or so behind them.

'What's he playing at?' murmured Dylan under his breath, but there was no one to hear him because Mari was already hurtling off after Gweeb. By the time Dylan caught up with her at the cliff edge, he was wheezing as heavily as if he'd just finished his first half-marathon.

'Worms, Dylan,' said Mari urgently, her eyes fixed on the dragon as he raced back and forth along the cliffs below them.

'What's he doing?' asked Dylan, peeling open the worm box.

'I don't know, but it's not the same behaviour as when he was chasing that sparrow,' Mari replied.

She cast a worried eye down the cliff path. In the distance, a man walking a chocolate-coloured Labrador was wandering in their direction. He hadn't seen them yet, but it wouldn't be long before he did.

Dylan thrust a worm into Mari's hands. She held it between her fingers and raised her arm high in the air.

'Gweeb!' she yelled. 'Come back!'

But Gweeb was far away now, diving low across the waves, then turning to swoop back up to the cliffs, and then out over the water again.

'It's almost like he's looking for something,' said Dylan.

'But what, though?' Mari wondered.

'And what if he doesn't come back?' asked Dylan nervously.

'Then I will blame you entirely,' said Mari.

The man and the Labrador were getting closer.

'Gweeb!' she shouted again.

'GWEEB!' they yelled at the same time.

Then, before they knew it, the Labrador was bounding up to them, sniffing Mari's jeans and jumping up at her outstretched arm. Mari shrank back, holding the worm out of reach while trying to avoid being slobbered on.

'Don't worry, he loves kids,' said the owner with a grin. He pointed at the worm Mari was still holding in the air. 'You'll not tempt that bat down with worms, you know. They're insectivores.'

'Thanks.' Mari grimaced, relieved that the man wasn't any more suspicious.

'Come on, Angus,' the man said to his dog as he kept on walking. 'You've got sheep to bother.' The Labrador came to heel immediately and trotted off behind him.

At almost the same moment, with no fanfare at all, Gweeb suddenly appeared, swooping down on to Mari's hand to take the worm like an obedient hawk. He curled his tail around her finger while he gulped it down in two swift movements.

'Good gwiber,' said Mari proudly, surprised to feel every inch the dragon trainer. 'Why did you fly off like that, eh?'

As Dylan leaned in to watch, Gweeb wheezed out his after-dinner breath into his face. Dylan gagged at the smell.

Mari giggled. 'Now that *is* interesting,' she said.

Dylan raised a questioning eyebrow.

'After feeding, his breath has the odour of rotten eggs,' she said.

'It certainly does,' said Dylan. 'Shall I write that down, Dr Jones?'

'Thank you, Assistant Dylan –' Mari smiled – 'but let's do that back at the farm. It's too risky to stay out here any longer.'

They picked up their things and placed Gweeb back in the reptile box. As Mari stole a last glance at the dog walker disappearing off along the path, the man blew a large plume of breath out into the crisp morning air. And a small but perfectly formed idea dropped into her head.

Chapter 13

Back in the kitchen, Mari was rummaging around in a drawer in the Welsh dresser.

'What are you looking for?' asked Dylan.

'I want to test a hypothesis,' she replied.

'Test a hippo-potheosis?'

'Hypothesis. A scientific theory. A starting point for investigation.'

'And your theory is?'

'Ha! There it is.' Mari brandished the lighter she'd just pulled out of the drawer.

'Hang on a minute,' said Dylan, looking worried. 'You said you would run stuff like this past me first.'

'Follow me,' said Mari. 'You bring Gweeb.'

But Dylan wasn't moving.

'Quickly,' said Mari. 'We don't have long before Mum gets back with the cows.'

Dylan reluctantly picked up the terrarium and followed her back out into the farmyard. Way off in the dairy, the milking machine was still making its familiar sounds.

'So, the rotten-egg smell . . .' said Mari. 'What do you think it means?'

'I don't know,' said Dylan. 'Gweeb's eaten some rotten eggs?'

Mari tried to be patient. Dylan wasn't a proper scientist, after all.

'No, it means that the dragon's stomach is producing some kind of gas as it digests its food. And this –' she held up the lighter – 'is going to prove it.'

'How?'

'I'm going to set light to it.'

'You're going to make Gweeb breathe fire?' Dylan looked horrified. 'Like in a fairy tale?'

Mari rolled her eyes. 'Yes, Dylan, and then I'm going to make him fight a tiny knight and kidnap a miniature princess.'

'Well, if dragons are real, maybe fairy tales are true too,' said Dylan.

There was no way a scientist like Mari was going to entertain that notion. 'We're not in a fairy tale, Dylan. We're in Wales. And Gweeb isn't a mythical creature, he's real. And I'm going to prove that he's breathing out methane by igniting the gas.'

Dylan instinctively pulled Gweeb's box close to his chest. 'I still don't think that's a good idea,' he said.

'All right, you can hold Gweeb,' conceded Mari. 'I'll do the science bit.'

Dylan grudgingly placed the box on the ground and removed the lid.

'Please feed him a worm, Assistant Dylan.'

He pulled a squirming worm out of the box. Gweeb's head snapped round towards him, tongue

lolling like a puppy begging for a treat, before snaffling the worm down. Standing behind them, Mari wasted no time in holding the lighter right next to Gweeb's gaping jaws.

'Too close,' warned Dylan.

Mari muttered to herself, and moved the lighter another ten centimetres away. As she did so, she heard a rumble in the creature's stomach and flicked up a flame. A second later, Gweeb belched out a stinky breath that instantly caught light, sending a tongue of flame shooting out about a metre in front of them.

'That is *so* cool!' said Dylan, grinning at Mari, who couldn't help but return the smile. Even Gweeb looked pleased with himself, his emerald eyes glinting.

'Hypothesis successfully proved,' announced Mari. 'Please write that down.'

'Shouldn't we do it again, just to be sure?' asked Dylan eagerly.

'Science before fun,' said Mari, pulling the ring binder out of her bag.

'Boo!' said Dylan as he put Gweeb back in the box.

'Dylan, the lid!'

Dylan had forgotten to close the terrarium, and that split second was all Gweeb needed. He sprang upwards, snatching the lighter out of Mari's hand with his claws as he whipped up into the air, flying across the yard, and high into the hay barn.

'You'd better be right about this training thing,' snapped Mari. 'Get another worm, quick. I've got to get up there.'

Dylan scrabbled around in Mari's bag, but the worm box was empty. He scratched about in the dirt beneath their feet instead, desperately trying to find something wriggling.

Meanwhile Mari cursed the fact that she hadn't stacked the bales properly yet. There was no way she could climb up the messy pile to get to Gweeb. She quickly began lifting, turning and slotting the bales into a tidy staircase of hay. It didn't take her long, and soon she was picking her way carefully upwards.

She glanced up at the tiny dragon, still perched way above her head. He was holding the lighter in one

claw like it was a toy, absent-mindedly scratching at it with the other. Mari felt her heart plummet. Sooner or later it would spark, and if that happened in a barn full of hay . . .

'Gweeb,' she called sternly. 'Put that down!'

He stopped what he was doing and looked over at Mari just long enough to make it clear both that he'd heard her and that he was going to ignore what she'd said. Mari craned her neck to see where Dylan was.

'Have you got a worm yet?' she shouted.

'I can't find any!' he yelled back.

'Try the old vegetable garden behind the house!'

Dylan nodded and ran off.

'From now on, new rules,' Mari muttered under her breath. 'The boy doesn't get to hold the dragon.'

She was a good five metres above the ground now, she realized nervously. But still Gweeb was out of reach. At the other end of the farmyard, the familiar squeezing and clonking sound suddenly stopped. Rhian had finished milking and would soon be going in for her breakfast. They were running out of time.

Mari looked back at Gweeb again – just as his claw struck the wheel and a flame spurted up out of the lighter. Mari held her breath, but unfortunately Gweeb didn't hold his. The little dragon wheezed – and a burst of flame shot across the barn.

Mari looked on in horror as the fire licked across one of the hay bales. It smouldered, then smoked, and then finally flickered into flame. Any second now, the whole barn would be on fire . . .

Chapter 14

'Dylan!' shouted Mari from the top of the hay bales. 'Worms! Now!'

But there was no sign of Dylan, and putting out the fire was now far more urgent than catching Gweeb. Edging warily back down to the ground, Mari scanned the barn and caught sight of a coiled hose in the corner. Racing over, she turned on the old tap and pointed the end of the hosepipe towards the growing flames. But the stream of water wouldn't reach. She looked out of the barn to see her mother walking up

from the dairy, driving the herd of cows in front of her. Mari's eyes instinctively flew back to the dragon, who had stopped flicking the top of the lighter and was now sniffing the air, clearly sensing the approaching milk source.

In a last act of desperation, Mari stuck her thumb over the end of the hose to squeeze the stream of water into a more powerful, concentrated jet. Finally it reached the burning bale and quenched the flames. Rhian hadn't seen her yet, but any moment now she would.

A plastic box came skidding across the stone floor of the barn and banged into Mari's foot. She looked down and saw that it was full of worms, then looked up to find out where it had come from.

'Hello, Mrs Jones, have you seen Mari?'

It was Dylan, stepping out from behind the hay barn to intercept her mother and the cows. Mari immediately dropped the hose, grabbed the box and thrust it in the air towards Gweeb. He instantly lost all interest in the lighter, dropping it on the

hay-strewn floor as he swooped down to gorge himself on the worms.

'*Pterodraco jonathani*,' Mari said. 'You are Trouble with a capital T.'

She bundled the dragon into the terrarium and firmly closed the lid, before hiding it with a great armful of loose hay.

'Mari! There you are!' said Rhian, spotting her. 'Look, Dylan's here.'

'Oh, hi, Dylan,' said Mari, appearing entirely uninterested.

'Mari . . .' said Rhian, raising her eyebrows as if to say, *Be nice to him*. 'What brings you round, Dylan?'

'We're, er, doing an experiment,' Mari said, before she really knew how she was going to end the sentence.

'OK,' said Rhian expectantly.

'Erm, it's for school,' Dylan said quickly. 'We're working together on a project. We're . . . partners.'

'Really? Mari didn't mention that,' said Rhian. Mari winced at how pleased her mum sounded. 'Well,

it's a shame, but Mari still has some farm work to do this morning and . . .'

Rhian's voice trailed off as she caught sight of the perfectly stacked bales in the barn. Mari enjoyed her small moment of victory.

'Oh,' said Rhian, a little bemused. 'In that case, why don't you both come in and have some breakfast before you start work?'

'Thanks, Mrs Jones,' said Dylan. 'That sounds lovely.'

'Thanks, Mrs Jones. That sounds lovely.'

Mari was doing a sing-song impression of Dylan talking to her mother. They were back in Mari's room, munching on fried-egg sandwiches while Gweeb polished off the few worms still left in the box.

'Hey,' replied Dylan. 'I saved your bacon back there.'

'Yes, well, I'm not sure my bacon needed saving, thanks,' said Mari. 'We just need to be a bit more careful.'

'Being in the farmyard rather than in the fields was already your idea of being careful,' said Dylan. 'And then Gweeb nearly burned the place down.'

'I *was* being careful, Dylan,' said Mari. 'I wasn't the genius who left the lid off the box.'

'OK, no, you weren't,' he admitted. 'But now we know more about Gweeb, we have to keep him away from things that can burn, like hay, and things with milk in them. Like cows.'

'Fine. So I'll keep him in my room. And, unlike some people, I'll remember to keep the top on the box and the door shut.'

Dylan shook his head. 'Keeping him cooped up in that little plastic box all the time is cruel. And he's clever – what if he does get out?'

Mari looked at Dylan sideways. She could tell he was working up to something. 'What exactly are you saying?' she asked.

'I'm saying he should be somewhere with more space. Where there aren't any cows. Or hay.'

Now Mari knew what he was getting at. 'With you, I suppose . . .'

'We're better equipped to look after him, Mari,' said Dylan.

'No,' said Mari, picking up the terrarium protectively. 'I don't think that's a good idea.'

'Mari, Dad has a proper terrarium in a shed in our back garden. It's where he keeps sick lizards and stuff. It's temperature controlled, has UV lights, and there's room inside for Gweeb to move around.'

'I need time to finish the tests,' said Mari. 'We still need to study Gweeb's sleeping habits. And his digestion. And we need to take pictures.'

'And we can still do all that – at my house,' said Dylan. 'And my dad has a camera.'

'But your dad would find him in there,' said Mari, still looking for any hole in the plan.

'Unless a poorly reptile comes in, he doesn't even go into the shed. And before you ask, no, we don't get many. Round here it's all cats, dogs and farm animals.'

'It's too risky,' said Mari. 'He should stay here. With me.'

'Seems like you're happy to take other risks. Just not this one. Are you worried you'll miss him too much?' said Dylan, with one eyebrow raised.

Mari bristled. 'I've told you, *Pterodraco jonathani* is not a pet. He is a major scientific discovery.'

'I think you're starting to care for an animal –'

'I am not!'

'Maybe you prefer living creatures after all,' said Dylan. 'You're becoming more like your mum.'

That was the final straw.

'Fine, Gweeb can stay with you,' Mari said. 'On two conditions.'

'Oh, so you have *two* conditions?'

She ignored him. 'Number one: you'd still be my assistant.'

Dylan held up his hands. 'You're the boss.'

'Number two: I want to see where you're going to keep him. I need to be satisfied that this place is suitable –'

'For *science*?' Dylan cut in.

'Exactly,' said Mari. 'For science.'

'No problem,' said Dylan. 'Let's go.'

Chapter 15

Apart from the driver, Mari and Dylan were the only people on the bus, but they weren't taking any chances – Mari had learned her lesson from the train journey to Cardiff. They sat right at the back, with Dylan's jacket over the travel terrarium to hide Gweeb from prying eyes, and Mari's arms resting heavily on top, so there was no chance of a reptilian escape. Even so, the journey into the village seemed to take much longer than usual. When their stop finally came, Dylan dinged the bell and they shuffled

down the aisle, each holding one end of the terrarium. Mari was relieved the trip had passed without incident.

'Cheers, Drive!' said Dylan as they climbed off the bus.

Mari shot him a look. They just needed to keep their heads down and get to . . .

'Hello, Dy-lan. What's in the box?'

It was Ffion, sitting at the bus stop, plucking chips from a bag.

'What's it got to do with you, Ffion?' asked Mari, irritated at being ignored.

'Oh, hello, Mari, nice to see you too.' Ffion gave Mari her fakest smile.

'Don't you need to get on the bus, Ffion?' asked Dylan, nervously trying to change the subject.

'Oh, I'm not waiting for it,' replied Ffion. 'It's just a nice place to sit, isn't it?'

As the bus pulled away, she jumped down from the bench and sidled up to Dylan. The colour seemed to drain from his face.

'So, what's in the box?' she asked again, sweetly.

Dylan's mouth opened and closed but no words came out.

'Must be very special,' she said, ducking down to try and sneak a peek. 'Why do you need the jacket on top?'

'We don't really have time to chat, Ffion,' Mari cut in. 'We need to get to Dylan's house.'

'Ahh,' said Ffion, popping another chip in her mouth. 'That sounds nice. Like a playdate?'

Mari could feel her blood boiling. 'You know they cook those chips in beef fat, right?' she said. 'Or did your dad tell you that's vegan too?'

Ffion's jaw froze mid-chew.

'It's a sick animal from Mari's farm,' blurted Dylan. 'We're taking it to my dad. He's a vet.'

Mari's heart sank. This was probably the worst thing he could have said. Ffion might always have been mean to Mari, but she adored animals.

'Oh no! Poor thing!' said Ffion, with real concern. 'What's wrong with it? Can I help?'

She put her hand on Dylan's shoulder, which made his face flush red. 'I could carry the box with you, if Mari is getting tired.'

'I am not in the least bit tired, thank you,' said Mari, taking the terrarium away from Dylan and cradling it in her arms.

'Well, at least let me walk with you,' said Ffion.

'Ah . . . OK,' agreed Dylan.

'What?' said Mari incredulously.

'Thanks!' Ffion beamed, slipping her arm through Dylan's.

'O-O-OK, great. Well, it's this way,' he said, pointing.

He set off with Ffion, leaving Mari to trail behind, simmering with anger. How could Dylan risk Gweeb being discovered, just for the chance to chat to Miss Glossy-Hair for five minutes?

'I suppose it's quite different from Cardiff here, is it?' Ffion asked Dylan.

'Cardiff's not all that.' He shrugged, throwing his head back to shake his fringe out of his eyes.

'Really?' said Ffion. 'It must be much more exciting.'

'Well, here's been pretty exciting so far, actually,' said Dylan.

'Not *that* exciting surely, Dylan?' said Mari through gritted teeth.

Dylan coughed. 'No, well, I mean . . .'

'So what *is* in the box then?' asked Ffion again.

'It's a snake,' said Mari loudly. 'A really big one. And it's *hungry*.'

Ffion turned to face Mari. 'Really?'

'Yep,' she continued. 'Dylan's dad is defrosting a dead mouse for it to eat.'

For a minute Ffion looked so shocked Mari thought she might throw up her chips. But she'd underestimated her.

'Oh, I *love* snakes!' squealed Ffion. 'Can I watch it feeding?'

'I don't know, Ffion, it's a bit gruesome,' said Dylan.

'Yes,' added Mari. 'Particularly for a vegan.'

'I *choose* not to eat animals, Mari Jones,' said Ffion with a patronizing smile. 'And I respect the fact that a

snake can't make that choice. Besides –' she turned to Dylan, sapphire eyes blinking up at him – 'I don't think I'd be scared if you were with me, Dylan.'

'Mari's going to help me today, Ffion,' said Dylan, puffing out his chest. 'But maybe another time?'

Mari glared at him.

'I wish *my* dad was a vet,' Ffion enthused.

'Yes, well, shame he prefers cutting animals up to curing them, isn't it?' said Mari. 'How far to your house, Dylan?'

'This is me actually,' said Dylan, stopping outside a white pebble-dashed house.

'Oh, OK,' said Ffion, her downcast look obviously fishing for an invitation.

'Snake's getting hungry, Dylan!' said Mari.

Dylan dug around in his pockets for his key but came up empty-handed. He gave another nervous laugh, and bent down to pick up a flowerpot by the front door.

'Ta-dah!' he said as he held up a spare key.

He unlocked the door, then replaced the key beneath the pot.

'OK, so maybe another time?' Ffion said to him.

'Yep, he'd love to. Bye!' said Mari, pushing past Dylan into the house.

'Bye.' Dylan waved a little stiffly to Ffion and followed Mari inside.

Mari kicked the door shut behind him. 'What do you think you're playing at?' she asked before Dylan had the chance to take a breath.

'I'm not playing at anything!'

'That awful girl is the last person you should be talking to right now.'

'She is not awful. She's nice and you should be nicer to her.'

Mari narrowed her eyes. 'You like her, don't you?'

'I do not.'

'You go all red when she talks to you.'

'That's not true.'

'I'm a scientist, Dylan. I observe things,' said Mari, pointing at his face. 'That's embarrassment triggering

your nervous system to widen the blood vessels in your cheeks. Makes them turn red.'

Dylan hurriedly tried to pat away the colour from his face. 'You just don't like her because she actually cares about animals. Like any *normal* person would.'

'Well,' she shot back, 'let's see how *you're* planning to care for Gweeb, shall we?'

Chapter 16

Dylan's house had been converted so that the ground floor was a veterinary surgery. It was closed on Saturday, so the house was quiet apart from the sound of barking somewhere at the back.

'Follow me,' said Dylan, leading Mari down the hall and into a long room with a series of pens along one side holding some of his dad's animal patients. They headed out of the back door to a large shed in the garden. Dylan yanked open the wooden-slatted

door and flicked on the light. An overhead fluorescent tube flickered on to reveal a dusty room filled with all manner of veterinary paraphernalia – cages, bags of food, medical equipment and, tucked away on a shelf at the back, a glass tank the size of a large aquarium. Dylan pressed a switch on the wall, and the box lit up to reveal a sandy floor, a few rocks and a dried-out log. He reached over to a nearby shelf to grab a jar full of mealworms and scattered some inside.

'And now,' he said, 'time to welcome Gweeb to his new home.'

'I'll do it,' said Mari quickly.

She prised open the travel terrarium to see that Gweeb was curled up asleep. Very gently she lifted him out and placed him in the terrarium, making sure the heavy lid was securely fixed. She pressed her nose up against the glass. Gweeb slowly raised his eyelids until the full majesty of his deep green eyes was revealed, then lazily stretched out his wings under

the heat lamp. Mari had to admit he looked quite content.

'Let's take some pictures,' she said.

'Here we go,' said Dylan, holding up a dusty black box with a huge lens, and straps sprouting from every corner.

'What on earth is that?' asked Mari.

'It's a camera. I think Dad got it as a birthday present once.'

'When? In 1986?'

'A camera is a camera,' said Dylan. 'It's even got film in it.'

'It's got *film* in it?' exclaimed Mari. 'What are we supposed to do with *that*?'

'When you've finished taking photos, you give the roll of film to the shop, and they hand you the pictures back the next day.'

'Good grief,' said Mari. 'What a waste of time. Are you sure your dad hasn't left a phone around?'

'This is as good as it's going to get.'

Mari shrugged. 'OK. Can you make it work?'

'Of course.'

Dylan fiddled with the lens, nearly dropping the camera in the process. He finally got it pointing in the direction of the tank, and started twiddling all the tiny dials and switches.

'Are you sure you know what you're doing?' asked Mari.

'Absolutely.'

Dylan turned the zoom lens so that it was fully extended and focused on Gweeb, then took a few steps back, steadied himself, and released the shutter with a satisfying click.

'Right,' he said. 'Will that do?'

'One picture?' said Mari. 'This is to illustrate a full scientific article. I'm going to need more than that. When I say so, take a photo.'

She reached inside the tank and stretched Gweeb out to his full length. 'Now,' she said.

Click!

Then she lifted his wings, placed him in the palm of her hand, and allowed him to twist his tail around her finger.

Click!

She ran through a few more positions, showing off Gweeb's crest and claws.

Click, click, click!

'That enough?'

'Just one more,' said Mari, lifting Gweeb out of the terrarium and holding him next to her cheek.

'Smile,' said Dylan.

'No, Dylan,' replied Mari. 'This picture needs to look like a scientist with the most important discovery they have ever made.'

She put on her most serious, grown-up face but, before Dylan could take the shot, Gweeb licked her without warning. His tiny tongue tickled her cheek and made her burst into a giggle.

Click!

'Perfect,' said Dylan. 'That's the end of the roll.'

Mari laid Gweeb softly back in the tank, where he returned to basking under the heat lamp.

'OK, I'll take the film to the photo shop,' said Mari, holding out her hand. 'Are you sure they won't look at the pictures?'

'Don't worry, it's all done by a machine,' said Dylan. 'But are *you* sure you're OK leaving Gweeb with me?'

Mari looked back at the little dragon. He seemed pretty comfortable, and the terrarium *was* more secure than her wardrobe.

'Yes,' she said. 'I suppose I am.'

Dylan handed over the roll of film.

'I should be getting home,' said Mari. 'Mum will be wondering why I'm not doing all the jobs she's asked me to do.'

'What are we doing tomorrow then, boss?'

'There's one last thing I need to know before I can write the article,' said Mari. 'What was going on down by the cliffs this morning when Gweeb flew off? What did that behaviour mean?'

'He was definitely looking for something,' Dylan replied.

'If he was,' said Mari, 'we need to know what.'

'But it's not safe to take him out on the cliffs again,' said Dylan. 'You said there were too many people around.'

'There's a cove at Llanwerydd Point,' said Mari. 'It gets cut off from the rest of the beach at high tide, but you can reach it by an old path. It's perfectly safe but no one goes that way any more.'

'Sounds like a plan,' said Dylan. 'See you tomorrow at . . . ?'

'High tide,' said Mari. 'Two p.m. On the cliff path that leads to the castle. Pick up the photos in the morning and you can bring them with you.'

She tapped on the side of the terrarium. 'Goodbye, Gweeb. See you tomorrow.'

To her surprise, he stretched out his tail to knock on the glass from the other side. She couldn't stop herself grinning.

'Strictly science with you two, is it?' said Dylan.

Mari didn't rise to the bait. 'See you tomorrow. Don't be late.'

Chapter 17

'What time is it, Mum?'

Rhian pulled her phone out of her back pocket. 'It's a quarter to two. You could wear that watch I gave you, you know.'

'Or you could get me a phone.'

'Hand me the pliers, please,' replied Rhian.

They were fixing the fence in the corner paddock. Or at least Rhian was. Mari was worrying whether she had enough time to get to Llanwerydd Point for

two o'clock, and whether Gweeb had survived his first night with Dylan.

'The pliers, Mari.' Mari pulled something out of the toolbox by her side and passed it to her mother, who let out a sigh. 'Those are wire cutters.'

'Here, sorry.' Mari handed over the pliers instead.

'Am I holding you up?' asked Rhian.

'I have to meet Dylan again. For the school project.'

Rhian raised her eyebrows. 'Well, you seem to be seeing more of the son than I am of the father.'

Mari grimaced. 'Could we talk about something else? Or maybe nothing at all?'

Rhian looked up. 'I'm sorry, Mari.' She seemed to be struggling to think of anything else to say. 'How's school?'

Mari groaned. 'Look, I have to go – now.'

'Can we talk about this whole thing tonight? Properly?'

'Do we have to?' said Mari. 'It's not going to change anything, is it?'

Rhian sighed, resigned. 'I suppose not, Mari. I suppose not.'

Mari started off across the paddock. Her mum called after her, 'Don't be back late. And watch the –'

'Tides. I know, Mum.'

Mari strode on without looking back. There was science to do. A future to build.

And a father to commemorate.

'Hang on a minute.' Mari was incredulous. 'You let Ffion into your house?'

She and Dylan were sitting on a rocky sliver of beach at Llanwerydd Point in the shadow of the castle. Gweeb was in his travel terrarium. The sea crashed in front of them.

'She said she came back because she was worried about the snake.'

'And you believed her?'

'Look, all I showed her were a few sick animals in the holding pens.'

'Oh, did you show her some wittle orphan kittens?' Mari opened her eyes wide and slow-blinked an impression of Ffion.

'That's all,' said Dylan. 'I told her she couldn't see the snake because it was too sick and needed to be kept on its own in the shed.'

'Well, I don't like it. And I don't trust Ffion.' Mari folded her arms.

'You're overreacting. She's nicer than you think she is.'

'So you keep saying,' said Mari. 'Do you at least have the photos?'

'Ah, yes,' said Dylan, wincing slightly as he handed over a small packet. 'I can explain –'

Mari let out a yelp of exasperation. They were all blurry. In most of them, Gweeb was nothing more than a red smudge, far too out of focus to show the all-important detail Mari wanted.

'I think I zoomed in too much,' Dylan explained.

'You don't say,' Mari snapped back.

'On the bright side, they gave me a memory stick with them on as well,' said Dylan. 'And look – this one's not too bad.'

He pulled out the shot of Mari laughing as Gweeb licked her face. It was the best of the bunch – Gweeb was at least a *dragon-shaped* blur – but it was hardly conclusive, and certainly not the sort of thing they put on the cover of the *International Journal of Science*. This was not the way she wanted to present her study to Dr Griff.

'It's not that bad,' said Dylan.

'Isn't it?' said Mari sharply, picking up Gweeb's box and getting to her feet. 'This is my big chance, Dylan. And you're kind of wrecking it.'

'Oh, I'm sorry,' said Dylan sarcastically, standing and grabbing the box from his side. 'You know what, I've changed my mind. I don't think we should be telling anyone about Gweeb. I'm worried about what'll happen to him.'

Mari pulled on the box. Dylan yanked it back.

'You mean, now *you've* already told someone about him?'

'I didn't tell *anyone*!' Dylan said angrily. 'What do you think they're going to do with Gweeb at the

Natural History Museum anyway? It's a place for *dead* animals. For specimens, not living creatures. If he's lucky, they'll ship him off to London Zoo to live in a cage for the rest of his life. If not, he'll be stuffed and mounted in a glass box.'

'They wouldn't do that!' snarled Mari, trying to wrench the box out of Dylan's hands.

'You don't know what they'd do! You're not thinking about Gweeb at all. You're only thinking about what *you* get out of all this.'

'It's not for me, it's for my dad!'

'Oh really? Are you sure?'

Mari was livid – perhaps because a part of what Dylan was saying rang true, and she didn't want to admit it to herself. With one final heave she snatched the box out of Dylan's hands, overbalanced, fell backwards and dropped the box on the rocks. As it hit the stones, the lid snapped clean off, and Mari and Dylan could only look on helplessly as Gweeb launched himself into the air and away.

'Gweeb!' they yelled in unison, but he was already picking up speed as he darted out to sea.

'Come back, *please*!' cried Mari. She turned to Dylan in panic, their argument forgotten. 'Get some worms!'

'Look! He's coming back,' replied Dylan.

It was true – before he'd gone very far, Gweeb had banked to the left, veering back to the beach, and was starting to turn circles in a bewildered circuit.

'He's doing the searching thing again,' said Mari. 'Now we can work out what for.'

But before they could get close, a seagull suddenly appeared from the clifftop and began harrying Gweeb. He whipped high into the air to avoid it, off in the direction of the castle, before disappearing out of sight.

Mari slumped. 'Now we're really done for,' she said.

'What do you mean?'

'That castle isn't just a castle,' she explained. 'It's a school. An international school, full of kids with

smartphones and Instagram accounts. If they see Gweeb, it won't just be the talk of Llanwerydd, it'll be right round the world in minutes.'

'Well, let's get him back before they see him then,' said Dylan, suddenly determined, as he offered his hand to Mari to help her over the rocks.

'What's that for then?' Mari looked down at his outstretched hand. 'I'd like to think I can climb over a rock by myself, Dylan.' He hurriedly pulled it away again. She smiled mischievously, accepting the temporary truce between them. Together they scrambled back to the stone cliff steps. At the top they came to a sea wall protecting the castle grounds from the elements, as well as from unwanted guests. A chain was strung across a gateway with a notice proclaiming NO TRESPASSERS. Mari climbed straight over.

'Are you sure this is OK?' asked Dylan.

'We're not trespassers,' said Mari. 'We're locals. Come on!'

Chapter 18

No sooner were Mari and Dylan through the gateway than a man appeared out of a building way off to their right, waving his arms. Mari ran left, ducking behind a boathouse. She fell against the wall, trying to catch her breath as Dylan caught up.

'Are you sure –'

But Dylan couldn't finish his sentence because Mari had already bounced herself back off the wall and was running towards the castle. He cast a look up to the heavens and raced after her. They snuck along behind

a few more school buildings before emerging on to a large sports field. Above them was the castle and, in between, a series of terraced gardens like a giant's staircase.

'Where do you think he's gone?' asked Dylan.

Mari looked skyward, searching for clues. A couple of seagulls were flying erratically up above the castle walls, darting back and forth as if they were chasing something . . .

'Up there!' she whispered, as loud as she dared.

They set off across the field towards a set of stone steps, but at the same moment the man who'd tried to stop them getting in appeared round the corner of the castle. They froze, hoping he hadn't seen them, just as a group of teenagers appeared out of one of the other buildings. Mari grabbed Dylan's arm and ran across to join the back of the group. She glanced nervously over her shoulder to see if the man had noticed, but he was still looking everywhere but at them. Meanwhile a pair of girls had turned to see who the two interlopers were.

'*Ils sont trop mignons, ces deux,*' said one, smiling at her friend.

'Eet is your boyfriend?' the other asked Mari in a strong French accent.

Mari put on the biggest smile she could muster, and threw an arm round Dylan. 'Please don't tell anyone you've seen us,' she said, tapping her nose with her index finger. 'It's a secret.'

The French girls tapped their noses in return and giggled. Dylan tapped his nose too, and laughed a little too loudly.

As the group climbed the steps, Mari craned her neck to try and catch a glimpse of Gweeb. When the teenagers reached the top and peeled away, Mari caught sight of the tiny dragon again, still wheeling in the sky, hotly pursued by the two gulls. She watched in horror as one of them seemed to catch Gweeb's tail, sending him tumbling towards the ground.

Mari gasped as he disappeared behind a high hedge, closely followed by the birds. She and Dylan raced up another set of steps into a rose garden – to see the gulls

pecking at a stone gargoyle set into one of the flowerbeds. As they ran forward, shouting and waving their arms, the startled gulls took flight, revealing Gweeb, who was trembling at the clawed feet of the statue. He whimpered and wheezed, flapping his wings to get away from them.

'It's me, Gweeb, it's Mari.'

She reached out a hand to comfort the dragon as he cowered behind the statue.

'I'm sorry, Gweeb,' she tried again. 'We'll look after you better. I promise.'

But he only shrank further away, nestling right up to the gargoyle, nuzzling against its stony face.

'I don't think he wants *us* to look after him,' said Dylan softly.

'What do you mean?'

'I mean,' said Dylan, 'I think I know what he's been searching for.'

'What's that?' Mari asked.

'He's been trying to get back to where he hatched . . . to find his family.'

Mari looked back at Gweeb. He seemed more vulnerable than ever. A tiny, gull-battered body, breathing heavily. She turned to Dylan again. 'But we have no evidence for that.'

'Look at the statue, Mari,' replied Dylan.

Mari did. And her breath caught in her throat.

The gargoyle wasn't a gargoyle at all. With a long, serpentine body, two stony wings and a pair of clawed feet, it was a dragon.

'Wait, you think Gweeb thinks this thing is, like, his mother?'

'It's possible,' Dylan replied.

Mari shook her head. 'It's a reptile, Dylan, not a baby. It's been chased by some predators and it's hiding behind a rock. It's just instinct. And pretty sensible it is too.'

Dylan's face darkened. 'Oh, it's an "it" again now then?' Not "he"? Not Gweeb?'

Mari rounded on him. 'What good is a mother to a reptile, Dylan? I'm sure I'd get along fine without one. And you don't seem to have needed one either.'

Dylan flushed as red as Gweeb, and pointed his finger at Mari. 'You speak for yourself, Mari Jones. You don't know anything about my family.'

He held out his hand to the dragon. Gweeb tentatively stuck his snout forward to sniff, before stepping cautiously on to it.

'He's not coming to you because he likes you more,' said Mari, flustered. 'You smell of food, that's all.'

'Whatever,' said Dylan, gently stroking Gweeb's scaly head with a fingertip.

'And don't think I'm letting you take him back after what you did.'

'It's still the safest place, and you know it,' said Dylan coldly. 'I'm taking him home now.'

'It's not his home,' said Mari. 'It's just the place you're keeping him.'

'And it's the best place to care for Gweeb.'

Mari's eyes were ablaze. Even if Dylan were right, she wasn't going to accept it. 'But he's *my* dragon,' she said firmly.

'Oh really?' said Dylan. 'Well, let's let Gweeb choose, shall we?'

'OK, fine,' retorted Mari.

Carefully, Dylan put Gweeb back on the gargoyle's head, pulled two worms out of the box and gave one to Mari. Then, like duelling gentlemen, they both backed away a few metres, and called out to Gweeb.

'Come to Mari, Gweeb!'

'Here, Gweeb!'

The dragon glanced from one to the other, looking completely befuddled by what was going on. The more they called, the more confused he seemed, twisting his head from side to side. Finally he sprang into the air, circled briefly above their heads, and then swooped down to take the worm Dylan was holding.

'There it is,' he said.

He took Gweeb over to the terrarium, lowered him in and picked it up. Mari watched as he retreated down the steps, and felt an unexpected sadness wash over her.

'Gweeb doesn't need anyone or anything,' she shouted after him. 'And neither do I!'

Back at Dimland Cross Farm, Mari pulled the battered old laptop out of its cupboard.

'I've got some homework to do, Mum!' she yelled as she ran up the stairs. 'I'll be in my room!'

While the computer spluttered into life, she pulled her binder of notes out of her bag and threw it on the desk. She flexed her fingers before opening a new document and typing in a title:

Pterodraco jonathani – *Discovery of a Flying Dragon*.

Mari's fingers flew across the keys, putting down everything she had learned about Gweeb in the few days she had been observing him. It wasn't until there was a knock at her bedroom door and she glanced at the clock that Mari realized she'd been writing non-stop for hours, entirely consumed by her article.

'I made you a sandwich, love' said Rhian, carrying a plate into the room. 'For your tea.'

'Thanks,' said Mari, turning back to the screen.

'What homework is it?' asked Rhian.

Mari stopped typing, unsure what to say. 'It's about what I want to do when I grow up.'

'Oh,' said her mum. 'Is it about farming?' she said, with a smile that said she wasn't serious.

But for Mari it didn't feel like a joke. 'Sorry, Mum,' she said. 'It really isn't.'

Rhian nodded, her smile fading, and backed out of the room without saying another word.

Mari's head dropped. She'd said the wrong thing, again. She pushed back her chair and went to her bedroom door. She should do something to make it right. But her mum was already halfway down the stairs and her phone was ringing.

'Hi, Gareth,' said Rhian as she picked up.

Mari shrank back into her room. Now was not the time. Not to mention the fact that she had an article to finish. She sat back down at her desk. With the text complete, she only had to add the photos. She plugged the memory stick into the laptop and found the picture of herself laughing at Gweeb. She paused for a

moment, glancing over at the circle of light cast by her desk lamp, wishing that the mischievous dragon was still basking underneath it. Then she set about cropping herself out of the picture. Finally she pasted the image into the article, and decided to have one last look through the photos to see if there was anything else she could use.

She leafed through the prints, shaking her head again at the terrible quality. But as she got to the end, one seemed oddly thicker than the rest. She bent a corner and realized it was two photos stuck together. She peeled them apart to reveal a hidden picture beneath. It must have been on the camera when Dylan picked it up.

It was a shot of Dylan as a baby, with Gareth, and a smiling black woman who must have been Dylan's mother. A happy family. A family that clearly no longer looked like that.

Mari wished she could take back what she'd said to Dylan earlier. She'd never found the right way to ask him why his mum wasn't around. She stared out of

the window at the darkening sky and thought about her dad. And how her family didn't look like it used to either.

Then she typed in an email address and attached the article.

'I'll make you proud, Dad,' she whispered.

And with that she pressed SEND.

Chapter 19

Black clouds were massing ominously in the sky as Mari walked from the bus stop to school the next morning. But she had purpose in her step. Great things were about to happen.

Across the way she saw the familiar yellow estate car pull up, and Dylan jump out, shirt untucked, school bag flailing. He came running over to Mari without even closing the car door.

'Dylan,' she said, 'I owe you an apology for yesterday. And I brought you this –'

She reached into her coat pocket for the picture of Dylan's mum, but before she could pull it out, Dylan interrupted. 'Gweeb's gone.'

Mari stopped in her tracks. 'What do you mean, "Gweeb's gone"?'

'I came down this morning and he wasn't in the terrarium.'

Panic started to rise in Mari's throat. 'What? How did he get out?'

'He didn't. Not by himself at least.'

'What do you mean?'

'The spare key. Under the flowerpot. She must have seen where it was.'

Mari clenched her fists tightly. Ffion.

'We need to find her,' she said. 'Right now.'

'She won't have brought Gweeb to school, will she?'

Mari shot Dylan a look of pure disdain. 'You mean, she won't have brought something into school that will gain her maximum attention and instant popularity? No, I'm sure she'd *never* do anything like that.'

'I-I'm sure there's an explanation,' stammered Dylan.

Mari got right up close and jabbed her finger in his chest. 'There's a very simple explanation. She's selfish, self-obsessed, and perfectly happy to put Gweeb's safety at risk for her own gain.'

Dylan glared back at Mari as raindrops starting pinging off their heads. 'Sounds just like someone else I know,' he muttered, though more than loud enough for her to hear.

Mari's eyes went wide as saucers, and she grabbed his jacket in both hands. 'She's. Not. Even. A. Proper. Vegan,' she hissed.

Before Dylan could reply, Mari was distracted by a commotion from the direction of the school, and looked over to see Ffion surrounded by a throng of friends. Mari pushed Dylan away and hared towards her, weaving through gaggles of students and dodging past a chain reaction of inflating umbrellas. She could see Ffion holding open a backpack for her best friend Isabella Reeves to look into. Isabella's face was a picture

of bewilderment, but before Mari and Dylan could reach them the bell sounded, and Ffion disappeared into the crowd of children funnelling into the school.

Mari and Dylan followed her to their classroom, where they found her already seated right at the front with her backpack hanging off the back of her chair. Mr Pugh was impatiently tapping his desk with a white-board marker.

'Nice to have you join us, Mari and Dylan,' he said.

Mari gave Ffion a dirty look as she took her seat right behind her. Ffion smiled her most angelic smile in return.

'Where is it?' hissed Mari.

Ffion didn't turn.

'Give it back!' Mari growled.

'Miss Jones,' said Mr Pugh. 'Is there something you would like to tell the class?'

'Ffion has something of mine, Mr Pugh,' said Mari. 'I was asking for it back.'

Ffion snorted. 'What could I *possibly* want of Mari's, sir?' she said.

The rest of the class started to giggle. Mari flushed crimson.

'All right, button it, everyone,' said Mr Pugh, beckoning a woman in a white coat into the class, 'because we've got a special treat for you today. This is Mrs Hashmi, the chemistry teacher at Llanwerydd Secondary,' he announced. 'She's come to give you a little taste of what lessons will be like in *big* school next year.'

'Oooooh,' said the whole class sarcastically.

Mari didn't join in. Her eyes were firmly fixed on Ffion's backpack, which had begun to twitch in a very familiar way.

'Thank you, Mr Pugh,' said Mrs Hashmi, holding up a purple sweet. 'Now, does anyone know what this is?'

Isabella's hand shot up. 'Jelly baby, miss!'

Ffion's bag twitched again, one strap slipping off the back of her chair.

'Yes, and this,' said Mrs Hashmi, picking up a test tube, 'is potassium chlorate . . .'

Mari nudged Dylan to get his attention.

'I'm putting it into this Pyrex tube, fixed to a stand at a forty-five-degree angle . . .'

Mari and Dylan watched, mesmerized, as a tiny but very sharp claw emerged from the side of Ffion's bag, moving backwards and forwards like a knife until it had torn a hole in the material.

'Now, this part is a little dangerous, so I'd like you all to put on the safety goggles you'll find on your desks . . .'

'Do something!' hissed Dylan.

'Like what?' Mari shot back.

They raised the goggles to their faces in unison as, through the hole, the unmistakable snout of a dragon appeared.

'And now I'm lighting a Bunsen burner beneath the tube . . .'

Following the snout came the rest of Gweeb, nosing the air, a tiny mealworm falling from his jaws.

'When the potassium chlorate is molten from the heat . . .'

Mari realized the danger immediately. If Gweeb had been eating, he would be full of flammable gas. Right in front of a naked flame.

'Ffion,' she whispered. 'He's getting out of your bag!'

Without turning round Ffion replied calmly, 'Sorry, Mari, it's *my* snake now.'

'Then we put the jelly baby into the test tube . . .'

Stretching out his wings, Gweeb climbed slowly to the top of the backpack, only a couple of metres from Mrs Hashmi's Bunsen burner.

'And here comes the surprise of your life!'

Gweeb opened his jaws wide, and Mari could see his belly quivering. There was nothing for it. She dived round the desk towards him.

At the very same moment Mrs Hashmi popped the jelly baby into the test tube, where it disintegrated with an extraordinary howl just as Gweeb blew out an enormous putrid breath towards the Bunsen burner. In a flash it was alight, sending a flare shooting across the classroom and setting fire to a flip chart.

Ffion screamed. The jelly baby screamed. Mari made a grab for Gweeb, but he was already up and away.

'What on earth?' yelled Mrs Hashmi. 'There's a bat in the classroom!'

Everyone in the class started screaming. Gweeb sent another methane-fuelled flame arrowing across the room, setting fire to a wall display and several shelves of textbooks.

'FIRE!' yelled Mr Pugh. 'Everybody out!'

The students all bundled for the door – apart from Mari and Dylan, who clambered chaotically around the classroom trying to bring Gweeb back down to earth.

'That means you too,' shouted Mr Pugh. 'OUT!'

'The window!' cried Mari, seeing that the one at the front of the classroom was partly open.

But it was too late. Gweeb darted past Mr Pugh and out into the playground beyond.

'Now really *out*, the both of you,' urged Mr Pugh, shoving them through the classroom door as the fire alarm started to reverberate around the halls.

'OK, everyone move SLOWLY and CALMLY to the exits please,' said Mr Williams, the PE teacher, holding out his arms to usher the throng of children down the corridor.

Mari and Dylan ducked under his reach.

'Oi!' he yelled. 'Mari Jones! New boy! I said SLOWLY and CALMLY!'

But Mari and Dylan were long gone, shoving through the rabble of students and past a shell-shocked Ffion, her blonde hair singed to a crisp. But there was no time to gloat over her comeuppance. They had a dragon to find.

Chapter 20

Out in the playground, gangs of children were goggling open-mouthed at the unfolding events. Despite the fact that it was raining hard now, flames were taking hold, licking up the outside of the school building. Mari and Dylan could hear their classmates muttering as they picked their way towards the sports field.

'Is school *properly* going to burn down?' enquired Angelo Thomas.

'With our luck, the rain'll put it out,' replied Geraint Sharma.

Mari and Dylan were the only ones looking in entirely the opposite direction, scanning the sky for any sign of Gweeb.

'Can everyone PLEASE line up in your classes!'

Mari and Dylan tried to look as inconspicuous as possible as Mr Williams attempted to take control in the playground.

'Mari Jones and Dylan Moss!' shouted Mr Pugh.

They turned round sheepishly.

'Right, that's two of you at least,' he said, turning away to look for the rest of his class.

'OK, now they know we're safe, let's go,' said Mari, pulling on Dylan's arm.

As they slipped out of the school gates, they heard the sirens of approaching fire engines, followed by the audible sounds of disappointment from their schoolmates. Mari looked up into the sky again, shielding her eyes from the falling rain.

'Where would you go if you were a frightened dragon?' asked Dylan.

'I'd probably go to the place where I last felt safe,' said Mari.

'And that would be the farm, would it?' said Dylan.

Mari's silence dared him to say different. But before either of them could say another word a shard of lightning illuminated the dark sky, making Mari jump. Electrical storms still made her very nervous, even six years after her dad's tragic accident. A low grumble of thunder followed as Mari noticed something over Dylan's shoulder.

'Bus!' she yelled, knowing it would be an hour before the next one.

She turned tail and pelted off towards the bus stop to catch it. Dylan swung his backpack over his shoulder and reluctantly loped after her.

Soon they were racing down the lane to Dimland Cross Farm and skidding to a stop in the farmyard, breathless and drenched.

'You check the barn,' Mari instructed Dylan. 'I'll see where the cows are. He might have gone looking for milk.'

'Why on earth aren't you two at school?' said Rhian, appearing through the back door of the farmhouse.

Mari and Dylan looked at each other, wondering how much they should say.

'The school's on fire, Mum,' said Mari.

'On fire?'

'It's true, Mrs Jones,' Dylan piped up. 'They've sent us all home.'

'Right, inside, the both of you,' said Rhian. 'You're soaked.'

'We can't, Mum,' said Mari, starting to squirm. 'We have to find the . . . thing that started the fire.'

'What *thing*?' said Rhian, narrowing her eyes. 'What have you done?'

'We haven't done anything, Mrs Jones,' said Dylan.

'Thank you, Dylan, but I was asking Mari,' replied Rhian.

Mari looked at her feet and felt the hard rain on the back of her neck. A fork of lightning scraped the sky, this time followed closely by a thunderous roar that made her shudder again.

'Come inside, Mari,' asked Rhian for the second time. 'You of all people know how dangerous it is.'

Deep down, Mari wanted nothing more than to come in out of the frightening storm, but that wasn't an option any more. It would mean giving up on Gweeb, on her dad and on her future. But could she really tell her mum all that? She took a deep breath.

'You're not going to believe this, Mum, but you have to trust me when I say that it's true,' said Mari.

Rhian cocked her head to the side suspiciously. Dylan looked from one to the other, bracing himself for what he now knew was coming.

'I found a dragon on the beach,' Mari announced. 'A tiny one. That's what set fire to the school. But now he's frightened, and I don't know where he's gone, but I have to find him before he gets hurt, or he hurts something else.'

Rhian stared back at Mari. The silence between them seemed to last an age.

'I see,' she said finally. 'Well, why don't we talk about this inside, out of the rain?'

'I know you don't believe me, Mum, but it *is* true,' said Mari. 'We need to go and find him right now.'

'What you *need* to do is come inside, Mari!' This time it was an order.

Mari stood her ground. 'I can't, Mum. I have to find Gweeb.'

Rhian suddenly snapped. 'OK, Mari. School sent you home? That I can believe. Because it's on fire? Maybe, just about. Because your miniature dragon tried to burn the place down? No. That's where I draw the line. That's where anyone who isn't mad draws the line. So what's really going on, Mari? Why are you lying to me?'

The storm was raging now. The rain pounded on Mari's head and the water streamed down her face. She looked her mum squarely in the eyes, and felt the frustration of six years bubbling up inside her.

'I'm not lying, Mum. *Please* listen to me. Dad would have listened to me.'

'Is that what you think?'

'I'm not like you, Mum. I'm sorry, but I'm not. I don't know about animals, or fixing fences, and I really don't want to be here all my life.'

'There's nothing wrong with –'

'I want to be a scientist, Mum, just like Dad. I'm doing it *right now*, and I'm sorry you don't understand, but I have to go. I can't let anyone stop me being who I want to be. Just like Dad told me.'

Rhian seemed to sway a little, like she'd been winded by a punch. Mari braced herself for her mum to yell at her, but she didn't. Instead she regained her composure and began to speak very calmly.

'Come inside, Mari. There's something you should know. Something I should have told you much sooner.'

'I can't, Mum. I need to go.'

Mari turned to leave. Gweeb could be in danger, She just couldn't have this conversation now. She grabbed Dylan's arm to pull him away.

'Your father isn't dead.'

It seemed so matter of fact, the way Rhian said it. Like she was talking about one of the cows on the farm, or a character on a TV show. Not at all like she was talking about Mari's dad.

'He wasn't struck by lightning, Mari. And neither were you.'

'But . . .' Mari turned round slowly to face her mum.

'You need to hear this, Mari. I'm sorry. The person who was struck by lightning was Mary Anning, not you. You read about it in a book when you were little, and it got into your head that that was what happened to you. I let you keep thinking it because it was better than the truth. Because he left us, Mari. When you were five. He didn't want to be a farmer any more, so he just walked out the door one night during a storm, and I never heard from him again.'

'But . . . but he was my dad . . .'

'I know, love. I don't know why he did it. I guess he wasn't going to let anyone stop him being who he wanted to be.'

Mari felt dizzy. It was like the earth was shifting beneath her feet. 'It's not true,' she said. 'It can't be true.'

'I wish it wasn't, Mari, but it is. Go and get your book on Mary Anning if you don't believe me. It's all in there.'

Mari's head was throbbing, because she knew instinctively that what her mum was saying was right. She knew it in her heart. And the truth hurt. It hurt a lot, and she knew she had to go now. Go and find Gweeb. Go and do something else. Somewhere else. Anything rather than face up to the shattering realization that her life was now completely and horribly different to what it was five minutes ago.

She ran off down the lane and Dylan followed, his school bag bouncing off his back.

'Mari!' It was her mum calling after her, but there was no way she could go back.

'Mari!' It was Dylan shouting now. 'Mari, wait!'

Finally she slowed to a walk, breathing too hard, too fast. She felt Dylan's hand on her shoulder.

'Are you OK?' he asked quietly.

She glared at him. Even though it was still tipping down with rain, tears were clearly slipping down her cheeks.

'Fair enough, stupid question,' said Dylan.

She was glad he was there all the same, even if she couldn't bring herself to tell him so.

Just then, a shiny black 4x4 pulled up on the road at the end of the lane, blocking their path. The window on the driver's side slid down with an electronic buzz.

'Is this Dimland Cross Farm?' said a familiar voice. 'I'm looking for Dr Jones.'

Chapter 21

Mari's eyes bulged. It was Dr Griff. *The* Dr Griff, in his trademark leather bomber jacket. Here at Dimland Cross Farm.

'That's her,' said Dylan, pointing at Mari. 'She's Dr Jones.'

Mari wiped the tears off her face to try and make herself look halfway presentable, though the storm had plastered her hair to her cheeks and her clothes were completely sodden.

'Well,' said Dr Griff. 'You're a little younger than I imagined from your email.'

He grinned, obviously pleased with his joke. Then his eyes narrowed. 'Hang on,' he said. 'You're the girl from the lecture last week, right?' He held up a sheaf of printed documents that Mari recognized as her article on Gweeb. 'Is this what you came to tell me about?'

Mari nodded sheepishly.

'OK, wow,' said Griff. 'Why didn't you say so?'

Mari cleared her throat. 'The creature. He wasn't well that day. I was worried . . .'

'Sorry, what am I thinking?' said Griff. 'You two look completely soaked.'

In a blink he'd jumped out of his car and thrown up a huge red golf umbrella over Mari and Dylan. It said *THE DINOSAUR HUNTER* in large white capital letters.

'Super cheesy, isn't it?' he said, smiling. 'But handy for weather emergencies.'

'The creature I wrote to you about . . .' Mari said.

'The dragon I found . . . It escaped. Dylan and I are looking for it now.'

Griff seemed a little sceptical.

'You do believe me, don't you?' asked Mari.

'The article was astonishing,' he said, 'but the photo *was* quite blurry.'

Dylan winced.

'I promise you it's all true,' said Mari, getting upset again. 'You *have* to believe me.'

Griff held her by the shoulders and looked her in the eye. 'I do, Mari, I do. You're a proper little Mary Anning. That's why I'm here.'

Mari felt herself relax. Here, finally, was someone who understood.

'Up there, look!' Dylan was pointing off into the distance towards the sea.

At first Mari couldn't see anything, the sky was so dark from the storm, but then, unmistakable against the breaks between the clouds, she spotted a tiny red body flying back and forth.

Dylan turned to Griff. 'I know it looks a lot like a bat from here, but –'

'No, Dylan,' said Griff, interrupting. 'Actually it doesn't.' He grabbed a pair of binoculars out of his glove compartment and held them up to his eyes. 'Body and wings too thin, prominent tail. Flying unusually high, in an undulating manner and –' he lowered his binoculars and beamed a knowing smile at Mari – 'in the daytime. Bit of a giveaway.'

Mari smiled back at him. She was in the company of a proper scientist. At last.

'I think he must be heading for the beach,' she told him. 'That's where I found him. Can you take us?'

'No time to waste!' he cried, flinging open the car doors.

Mari jumped straight into the front seat. Dylan looked a little more reluctant.

'Shouldn't we ask your mum?' asked Dylan.

'Worried about stranger danger, kiddo?' Griff asked him. 'Don't worry – you know me from the telly.'

'Get in, Dylan!' yelled Mari.

'Just mind those muddy feet,' Griff told Dylan with a wink. 'Leather's a devil to clean.'

Dylan reluctantly swung himself up into the back and buckled his seatbelt.

'OK, Mari,' said Griff. 'You're in charge. Tell me where we're heading.'

The rain was lashing against the windscreen so hard that the wipers were struggling to keep up. Griff strained forward to try and make out the road ahead. They were following a winding, rolling track that eventually led them on to the clifftops by the lighthouse.

'Stop here,' said Mari.

Griff did as he was told. He pulled up on a grassy verge and they piled out. Griff attempted to put up his umbrella, but the powerful wind off the sea flipped it inside out almost immediately. Awkwardly he wrestled it closed and threw it straight back into the car. Mari was already halfway down a steep grassy bank that sloped to the stony beach. Dylan was doing his best to follow, but the ground was pockmarked

with ankle-turning dents and he had to take care not to trip. Mari had no such worries. Her feet knew their way without her even looking. She was entirely focused on the sky.

'I can see him!' she yelled over the blowing gale.

She didn't wait for the others to catch up, but forged ahead, bounding over the slippery round stones on the beach. She could see Gweeb, diving and weaving along the cliffs like a low-flying jet. He seemed agitated, and the closer she got, the further away he seemed to fly. Eventually Griff caught up with her, smoothed back his wind-tousled hair and raised his binoculars again.

'It's this searching behaviour I don't understand,' said Mari. 'He seems to be drawn here, but I don't know why.'

'It certainly doesn't look like hunting behaviour,' said Griff. 'Or play. But I would need to observe it for longer to be sure.'

Then Gweeb disappeared round a headland off to their left. They waited, but he didn't reappear, so Mari and Griff gave chase, Dylan panting behind them.

The tide was coming in, and when they got to the headland they had to wade through water half a metre deep to see round the jutting cliff. It wouldn't be long before the shallow cove they were entering was cut off entirely. It was a narrow strip of shingle, pressed up against a sheer cliff that must have been thirty metres high. There was no sign of Gweeb, but in the middle of that cliff, about a hundred metres away, they could see a large, dark cave, partially hidden by a fresh rockfall.

'He must have gone in there,' said Mari, pointing to the forbidding hollow.

'We can't follow him,' Dylan said. 'The rocks look unstable, and the tide could trap us in there.'

'Then it could trap him too,' Mari told him. 'We have to go after him.'

'He can fly out when he sees the water coming in,' replied Dylan. 'We can't.'

'You don't have to come,' said Mari. 'I've got a proper scientist to help me now.'

Dylan stood firm. 'Tell me one thing: are you going in there to save a friend or retrieve a specimen?'

Mari glared back at him until Griff broke the tension.

'Let's just get it back, shall we?'

'Yes,' replied Mari. 'Let's.'

Chapter 22

As Mari and Griff started towards the cave, Dylan let out a growl of frustration and followed, nervously eyeing the onrushing sea.

'Have you got your phone?' Mari asked Griff as they reached the mouth of the cave, picking their way over the loose rocks.

Griff looked confused for a second, then realized what she meant. He flipped on his phone's torch and illuminated the chasm. The cave wasn't terribly wide, or all that tall – probably three times Mari's

height — but it was very deep. Staring into the darkness, even Mari started to have second thoughts about going any further, but she swallowed her fears and pushed on, with the others in hot pursuit.

By the light of the shaking phone, Mari could finally see where Gweeb had got to. He was flapping around at the back of the cave, scrabbling against one of the stony walls. She tried to reach out and catch him, but he was too quick and too slippery.

'Gweeb,' she urged. 'Come here.'

Mari could hear the waves crashing behind them. She didn't need to look to know that the sea was almost at the mouth of the cave. Another few moments and they would be cut off.

'We're trying to get you out of here,' she pleaded.

But Gweeb didn't seem to have any intention of leaving.

'He won't come to me, Dylan,' said Mari. 'I don't think he trusts me.'

'Stop trying to catch him, and let him come to you,' he said.

'We don't have time for that!' cried Mari. 'I'm just no good with animals. You do it.'

'No, Mari,' said Dylan. 'He's your dragon. He will come to you.'

Mari swallowed her exasperation and, against her instincts, stood still. Gweeb stopped flapping and perched on a nook in the rock, looking down at her.

'I don't have any worms, and I know I'm no good at this,' Mari said. 'But I'm asking you to come back to me. Please.'

Gweeb eyed her warily. Then, after what seemed like an age, he hopped off the rock, flapped lazily on to her palm and curled his tail around her finger.

Mari let out a breath that turned into a delighted laugh. 'Welcome back.'

'Oh my God,' exclaimed Griff. 'It's beautiful.'

In the light from the phone, Gweeb's crest shone as if it were a prism. Almost as if he knew he was on display, he stretched out his wings before tucking them contentedly back against his body.

Griff's eyes were on stalks. 'It really is . . .' He couldn't quite bring himself to say it. 'I mean, it just shouldn't be, but it absolutely is . . .'

'A dragon?' said Dylan.

'A dragon,' Griff finally confirmed.

Mari smiled again, this time with the pride of knowing beyond a shadow of a doubt that she had discovered something truly amazing. And that one of the people she most respected knew it.

'Can I hold him?' asked Griff.

'Come on, guys, let's do the dragon-handling later – we need to go now,' said Dylan, glancing anxiously behind him.

But Mari wasn't going to miss out on her moment of glory. She turned and extended her hand towards Griff, who reached forward with his and watched, captivated, as Gweeb made a twisting little journey from her finger to his. Griff brought the dragon up close to his face, his other hand holding his phone to illuminate the scene. His eyes grew wide with joy as he looked from Gweeb to Mari.

'This is going to change everything,' he breathed.

Mari felt all the bad feeling just melt away. Griff was right: whatever had gone before – with Dylan, with her mum – it was in the past now. Her life was finally going to change for the better.

Meanwhile Griff was performing a rather close inspection of Gweeb's underside. 'I should tell you though,' he said, 'that I suspect Gweeb isn't a boy dragon. From what I know of the biology of the closest reptilian cousins, *he* looks more likely to be a *she*.'

Mari raised one eyebrow in Dylan's direction, and he shrugged back with a slightly sheepish smile.

'You've done brilliantly with her, Mari,' Griff said. 'But this is too important to keep to ourselves. It's time to tell the world about Gweeb.'

'Yeah, well, we won't be able to tell anybody if we drown in here!' said Dylan.

Mari and Griff turned to see the water lapping inside the cave. They were seconds away from being cut off by the tide.

'Let me just get a picture of her,' said Griff, holding up his phone.

But there wasn't time for that: before anyone had a chance to say another word, there was an almighty rumble above their heads – not from the sky, but from the earth.

With an apocalyptic crash, the entire mouth of the cave collapsed and everything went black.

Chapter 23

The first thing to return was the sound of the waves, as far away as someone else's dream. Then a lightning crack and the rumble of thunder getting closer. One one thousand, two one thousand, three one thousand. And then, finally, the driving rain against the rocks. But, as Mari slowly opened her eyes, there was still no light to see by.

She could feel cold, wet stone beneath her cheek and knew that she must be lying down, knocked there by the rockfall. She stretched her arms and legs

fearfully, to be sure that her body was working properly, and was relieved to find that it was. She lifted her head and levered herself into a sitting position.

A flash of light suddenly illuminated the space from what seemed like a pinprick high up above her head. Although she was dazed, Mari could still work out what must have happened. The mouth of the cave had been covered by a huge rockfall, and only a tiny hole was left at the top of the slide. Not even big enough for a child to crawl through.

'Dylan! Dr Griff!' she shouted above the sound of the waves. 'Gweeb!'

Another lightning flash enabled her to see what was happening. Dylan and Dr Griff were both flat out on the floor of the cave, and Gweeb was licking Dylan's ear, in what seemed to be an effort to wake him up. Mari crawled over and shook him gently. Dylan moaned, and flipped over on to his back. He looked up at Mari as the lightning hit again.

'What . . . happened?' he murmured.

Mari smiled, glad to find that he was OK. 'Stray chips,' she said. 'Big ones.'

'Urghhhh . . . Ow!' came a voice from the other side of the cave.

'Dr Griff? Are you OK?' called Mari.

'Can't . . . move . . . my . . . leg,' came the pained response.

As they scrambled over to Griff, Mari slipped on something smooth and fumbled around in the dark for it. Griff's phone. Mari could feel where the screen had cracked, but it was intact. She prayed that it still worked. She found the phone's torch function and flicked it on to reveal Griff's leg: it was trapped at an awkward angle beneath a large rock. Dylan leaned forward to grab it, but Mari pulled him back, remembering the incident with the calf. She wasn't going to make the same mistake twice.

'It might be broken,' she said. 'We have to be careful not to move him. Help me lift the rock.'

Mari put the phone down with the torch facing upwards so there was enough light in the cave to see

by. Then, together, they very carefully raised the rock off Griff's leg.

Griff blew through gritted teeth in pain. 'Call an ambulance,' he said tightly.

'There's no phone reception down here,' said Mari.

'Then how are we going to get out?' Griff snapped irritably.

Mari had been so concerned about everyone being OK that the realization that they were trapped was only just sinking in.

'Er, guys,' said Dylan, pointing. 'Is that water coming in?'

Sure enough, seawater was seeping into the cave through the rockfall. Mari knew what that meant. It meant the tide was still rising and the rockfall wasn't watertight. They had less than an hour before high tide, when the cave would be entirely reclaimed by the sea.

Mari desperately tried to think of a solution as Gweeb flapped at her ear, just as agitated by the situation as she was. She tried to brush him – her – away so she could concentrate.

First she had to check if there really was no way out. Mari climbed up the loose rocks towards the little chink of the outside world that was still visible. Small stones broke and rolled beneath her feet as she scrambled to the top.

'Watch out!' cried Dylan as some of the debris landed centimetres away from him.

Shrugging an apology, Mari peered out through the small gap that had been left by the collapse. She could see the storm still raging outside, a sky-scraping piece of forked lightning hitting the water in the distance. She tried to pull at the rocks around the hole to make it bigger, but they were large and heavy.

'Help me, Dylan,' said Mari, knowing that Griff wasn't going to be of any use.

Dylan clambered up the slope to join her, and together they grabbed hold of one of the limestone blocks and managed to heave it out of the way. Others followed, one by one.

'OK, that's enough,' said Mari after a few moments. 'I think I can fit.'

Pushing her arms ahead of her, she wriggled forwards until the top half of her body was through to the outside. And then Mari realized the full extent of their predicament.

All she could see was the sea. The tide was rising by the second, waves already crashing right up against the rockfall. There was no beach anywhere to be seen, and no way to escape. Even if they could get out of the cave, it would be very dangerous to try and swim back to the shore – the currents were too strong and the sea too angry. They would be smashed back on to the rocks. The only possible way out was by boat, but no one was crazy enough to be out on the sea in this storm. No one would be looking for Mari and Dylan, because no one knew where they were, and there was no way of getting a message to them. Unless . . .

Of course! *That* was the answer.

'Pull me back in!' Mari shouted to Dylan.

She felt the tug on her ankles and let herself be hauled back into the cave.

'There's no way out,' she said breathlessly. 'The tide's already too high. But . . . do you still have your school bag with you?'

'Yes, but –'

'I need a piece of paper and a pen.'

'What for?' asked Dylan.

'Just hurry!'

He scrabbled in his bag and found what Mari was looking for. Mari quickly tore at the page until she had a piece of paper that was no more than five centimetres square. Then, very carefully, she scribbled something on it. When she'd finished, she pulled a hair tie from her ponytail and held out her hand.

'Here, Gweeb,' she said. The dragon swept down from her perch on the cave wall and landed on her finger. Mari rolled the piece of paper around her tail, fixing it tight with the elastic hair tie. Then she brought the dragon up to her face and looked her in the eye.

'Take this to Mum, Gweeb. On the farm. Where the cows are.'

'What are you doing?' said Griff incredulously. 'That's a wild creature, not a homing pigeon.'

'As a scientist, I would have said the same thing,' said Mari. 'But now I know what an extraordinary animal Gweeb is. Dylan helped me to see that.' She smiled at her friend. 'I think she knows we need help.'

'Once it's out of this cave, you'll never see it again,' Griff snapped. 'At least let me take a photo first.'

'No time for that,' replied Mari, rooting around in her own bag for one of the milk pots left over from the train. She peeled back the lid and gave Gweeb a drink, hoping it would give her the energy she needed to battle her way through the lashing rain. Then she lifted Gweeb up to the hole in the rock.

'Find Mum, Gweeb,' Mari said, releasing the dragon into the storm.

For a moment Gweeb seemed uncertain, buffeted by the wind as she circled round the opening, almost as if she didn't want to leave. Lightning smashed down over the sea behind her, lighting up the whole cove. Gweeb had never looked so tiny, never seemed more

vulnerable, than she did now against this vast, angry sky. Mari suddenly panicked that she was putting Gweeb in terrible danger. But then, as if making her mind up, Gweeb spread her wings wider and turned, flying headlong into the storm.

Chapter 24

Seawater was covering the floor of the cave now, and swirled threateningly against Griff's feet. Mari and Dylan had managed to lift him up on to the rocks, above the rising water, but it was creeping ever closer. Mari was stationed by the opening, scanning the horizon for any sign of help. Just below her, Dylan lay back with his eyes closed, as if he could will their predicament away.

'I'm getting wet again,' whined Griff.

Mari and Dylan scrabbled over and did their best to lift him, but it was difficult without sliding on the loose rocks beneath their feet. Mari staggered under his weight and slipped as a stone gave way.

Griff cried out in pain. 'Watch out!' he barked.

Mari looked down to see the smooth rock that had failed to support her. Something seemed different about it, but the light was still far too low to make it out.

'I'm going to need the torch,' she said.

Dylan fumbled around for Griff's phone, and handed it to her. She directed the beam down at the rock. It was rounded, and in the torchlight she could clearly see its reddish hue.

'It can't be . . .' she murmured.

'Can't be what?' asked Griff.

Mari swung the light around the cavern. She jumped across the rockfall, stopping every now and then to examine the debris more closely. 'I can't believe I didn't notice this before!' she cried.

'Notice *what*?' said Griff, his irritation building.

Mari directed the beam of torchlight at reddish round rock after reddish round rock, all poking up out of the rubble. '*This* is what Gweeb has been looking for,' she said. 'This is why she's been acting so strangely whenever she's near the beach.'

'WHAT IS IT?' yelled Griff.

'Eggs,' Mari replied. 'All these red rocks are eggs. Just like the one Gweeb hatched out of. The rockfall has released them.'

Griff's eyes bulged with excitement. 'Bring one to me!' he shouted. 'Quick!'

Dylan passed one to Griff, who held it up and turned it from side to side. And then he began to laugh. It started as a chuckle, but as it went on it became more and more bitter.

'You're right,' he said. 'Eggs. A whole new species. And here we are, about to drown. I never thought that the biggest day of my life would also be my last.'

'We're getting out of here,' said Mari, with complete conviction. 'Gweeb will find a way to get help. I know she will.'

'It's not coming back and we all know it,' snarled Griff.

Dylan looked shocked, but Mari wasn't giving up that easily.

'Thinking like that isn't going to help us either, Dr Griff,' she said.

But Griff was just getting going. '*Dr "Griff" Griffiths*,' he said, as if he were reading out the news, '*star of TV's* Dinosaur Hunt, *died today while fossil hunting on a beach in Wales. Although liked by some children, he was never much of a scientist, and never discovered anything important.*'

'They wouldn't say that, Dr Griff,' said Mari.

'You don't think so? What exactly would you know about it?'

'What about all the children you've inspired?' replied Mari hotly. 'All my life I've dreamed of being a scientist like you.'

Griff half coughed, half spluttered out another laugh. 'Well, welcome to the real world, Mari Jones. Where even if something good happens to you, it'll

turn bad before you blink. This should have been the discovery that made me famous.'

And with that Griff raised the egg he was holding high above his head and brought it crashing down on to the rocks next to him. The egg cleaved instantly in two – to reveal a tiny, dusty creature within it. Griff snatched it up by the tail.

'What are you doing?' shouted Mari in horror.

'I,' said Griff, 'am making the best of a bad situation.' He scooped some water up from beneath his feet and anointed the dragon with it. 'I name thee *Pterodraco griffithsi* – Griffiths' Flying Dragon!'

The dragon he was holding twitched into life, twisting and turning away from his finger.

'But that's Mari's discovery, not yours!' shouted Dylan.

He made a grab for the dragon, but as he did so he leaned against Griff's broken leg. Griff let out a scream of pain.

'The dragon!' shouted Mari. 'Be careful of the dragon!'

The tiny creature Griff had been holding wriggled free of his hand and flapped erratically across the rocks. Mari tried to catch it, while Griff held Dylan off.

'You are *children*!' yelled Griff. 'You don't deserve to make *discoveries*. I've spent the last fifteen years of my life grinning into a camera, surrounded by grubby little oiks like you. Do you know who takes me seriously? No one! I could have been Sir David Attenborough. I could have had a knighthood too. I could have had *respect*! But *I* don't get invited to the Palace – oh no – *I* get invited to play Buttons in the Swansea Christmas panto.'

Griff manhandled Dylan to the ground and picked up another egg, smashing it down and breaking it apart. He dragged himself painfully across the rocks to crack another and another.

'Stop it!' yelled Mari. 'You're going to hurt them!'

All she could think about were the vulnerable little animals flopping and flapping around them in the dark like baby turtles.

'I'm giving birth to them!' cried Griff. 'I, Dr Griff, am giving them *life*.'

Mari reached down into the water to scoop up a tiny dragon that was struggling to stay afloat. 'But they can't swim! They'll drown in here with us!'

'Then that will be my legacy,' cried Griff, with a sparkling madness in his eye. 'They will find my bones next to the remains of a brand-new species. And they will surely name it after –'

'Mari,' announced Dylan, knocking Griff out cold with the rock he was now holding.

'Dylan!' yelled Mari. 'What did you do that for?'

'He was going crazy,' he said. 'He was going to drown all the dragons.'

'And smashing him over the head with a rock is the answer?'

'Well, it's *an* answer . . .'

'You're as bad as each other, you boys. Thank goodness Gweeb is a girl. We might actually have a chance of getting out of here alive.'

Chastened, Dylan leaned down to feel Griff's pulse. 'He'll be fine. I didn't hit him very hard. He'll have a bit of a sore head, that's all.'

'Help me collect up all the dragons,' said Mari. 'We need to get them as far away from the water as possible.'

Working quickly, Dylan and Mari picked up the confused and frightened reptiles and popped them carefully into his backpack. A few flapped their wings as if they wanted to fly, but they were too dazed from their hatching.

'You do realize you've got a whole species in your school bag?' said Mari as she slipped the last one in.

'It's not even a very big bag.' Dylan smiled. 'Now what?'

'We wait for Gweeb,' replied Mari. 'That's all we can do.'

Chapter 25

The water was considerably higher in the cave now. Mari could no longer stand up without hitting her head on the roof. She wriggled out through the hole to look for any sign of help, but only got a mouthful of sea spray for her trouble. The waves were crashing just below the opening – and, what was worse, she could see the powerful current dragging some of the loose material away from the rockfall. Any minute now the pile of stones that was holding them up above

the waves might collapse and throw them headlong into the sea.

Mari squinted through the rain at the empty horizon and felt a lump rise in her throat. She watched a fork of lightning crack into the sea in the distance. She realized it no longer made her flinch – though it still made her think about her dad. About all those times she'd wished he were with her. But now she knew that he could have been if he'd wanted to. It was almost too much to bear.

She scrunched her eyes up tight to hold back the tears, and for once it wasn't an image of her dad that came into her mind. It was an image of her mum in their kitchen, holding a cup of tea in both hands, staring out of the window at the beating rain, worrying where her daughter was. She would be fearing the worst, just like she always did. And this time she would be right.

More like a prayer than a plea, she whispered, 'I really need you, Mum.'

A distant grumble of thunder cut her imagining short, but still she dared to believe that Gweeb would

find Rhian, and Rhian would find them. Because they *had* to.

Thinking of her mum reminded Mari of something, and out of her pocket she pulled the crumpled photo of Dylan and his family she'd found among the ones of Gweeb. She ducked back inside the cave.

Griff was still unconscious, only his head and torso now above the water. Dylan was huddled on the last tiny patch of dry rocks, clutching the backpack of dragons to his chest.

'Here,' Mari said, handing him the photo. 'This is what I wanted to give you this morning. It was on the roll of film in your dad's camera.'

Dylan stared at the photo like it was a priceless treasure. He took a deep, shaky breath.

'It's your mum, right?'

He nodded. 'She died when I was little. I never really knew her. It hurts Dad too much to talk about it and I don't have many pictures of her.'

Mari nodded. She knew how he felt. Or at least she used to know.

'I thought I knew my dad,' she said. 'I didn't think there could be anything worse than him having died. But now? Now I'm not so sure.'

Dylan put a hand on her shoulder. Mari looked down at the water lapping against her feet.

'I don't suppose any of it matters any more,' she said.

But then, out of the deluge, a tiny dragon swooped into the cave and crashed into her chest.

'Gweeb!' cried Mari.

The note was missing from her tail. Surely that meant . . . ? Mari swung round to look out to sea, but there was nothing. No sign of rescue, only waves smashing against the rocks below.

Mari began to laugh and cry at the same time. However grateful she was to see Gweeb, she knew now that their last hope of rescue was gone. She looked over at Dylan, and she could tell that he knew it too. She glanced down at the tiny red dragon nestling in her hands, panting heavily with the effort of flying against the storm.

'I know you did everything you could, Gweeb,' said Mari. 'Thank you.'

She lifted her up to the weak light filtering in from outside, and remembered the moment she had first held her, marvelling at this creature and everything that her existence meant for the world, for herself and for her dad. But that wasn't important any more. She certainly didn't care about Latin names, or what her dad would have thought. The only thing that was precious to her now was life. And even if hers and Dylan's were lost, there was no need for this beautiful animal to perish with them. Above all else she wanted her to be safe. She wanted Gweeb to be where *she* needed to be.

'I think we found what you've been looking for,' she said to the dragon.

Dylan unzipped his bag to reveal the mass of little red, winged reptiles inside. He laid it gently down on the rock so that they could crawl out.

Gweeb's head pulled up sharply when she saw what was happening, like a dog seeing a squirrel scamper

across its path. Mari slowly lowered her down to meet her relatives.

'It's your family, Gweeb,' she said.

Gweeb edged forward, her snout sniffing the air. Another dragon with a yellow stripe above its eye crept forward to meet her until their noses were almost touching. Mari and Dylan watched awestruck as the dragon's long tail curled round towards Gweeb. Gweeb's own tail slid along the rock to meet it, until one began to entwine with the other, twisting round and round until they were locked together in a reptilian embrace.

And then, as quickly as they had made the connection, their tails untwined in the same way. Gweeb, transfixed by her double, remained rooted to the spot. The yellow-striped dragon turned to see the others streaming out of the bag, and began to stretch its wings – slowly at first, then with more power, testing their strength. It began to lift off, pointing its snout towards the light, and then, with a flick of its tail, it flew through the hole towards the sea. The dragons that had followed it out of

the bag instantly gave chase. One by one they streamed out of the hole until only Gweeb was left. The tiny dragon looked up at Mari, as if asking for permission.

'It's OK, Gweeb,' she said. 'They're your family. You should be with them.'

Gweeb picked her way across the little patch of rock towards Mari, and twined her tail around her finger. Their eyes met for a moment, then Gweeb turned to face the light. She crouched down, preparing to spring off and away.

'No!' A hand clawed around Gweeb, pinning her down. 'You're not going anywhere! This is my discovery. My legacy!'

'Let her go!' yelled Mari, desperately trying to prise Griff's fingers off Gweeb's body. Dylan joined in, wrestling him from behind.

'I. Won't. Let. Go!' growled Griff through gritted teeth.

'You will!' Mari yelled back. 'She is no one's discovery! She deserves to be free!'

Then suddenly a lot of things happened at once: the almighty swell of a wave, a grating, sucking noise as

rocks were pulled across rocks, the ground shifting under their feet, and an inrushing of light as the stones beneath them fell away. The sea was taking back the cave. There was no stone beneath them now, only water, rushing, swirling, pushing them.

Gweeb sprang into the air as Griff loosened his grip – though she couldn't leave Mari and Dylan to their fate, and stayed, hovering above them, too small to help. Mari struggled to keep her head above the surface as she was sucked under, then spat back up, then sucked under again. There wasn't time to think, only a welcome flash of understanding that Gweeb was safe.

Mari tried to swim to safety, but the current was too strong, the waves too angry and the rocks too jagged. She caught sight of Dylan, rising and falling in the swell next to her, a look of panic in his eyes. She managed to stretch out and touch his hand, just for a second, before a wave swung him out of reach. Too late. It was all too late . . . She was going under.

'Mari!'

Mari couldn't see where the voice was coming from, but she recognized it instantly. Was she dreaming, or was it real this time?

'MARI!'

It was *her*. It *had* to be her.

A surge of energy lifted Mari up, and she saw a small rigid inflatable lifeboat coming round the headland with two people on board.

'MUM!' she screamed back, kicking towards the boat with every ounce of strength she had.

But the boat was rising and falling in the swell, and Mari was still sinking. The noise and colour of the world disappeared and it wasn't returning. There was no way to get back, only sucked-under nothingness.

And then, at her last breath, a hand was gripping her arm, and the strength of it was pulling her up out of the sea. Rhian.

Her mother was saving her life.

'I've got you,' was what Mari heard her mum telling her. And with it Mari felt relief, and love, and regret.

'I'm . . . sorry,' she spluttered.

'No,' said Rhian, drawing her daughter close. '*I* am.'

Mari and her mother held each other tightly. Enough to try and wring out all the hurt.

'Dylan!' It was Gareth, at the front of the boat, hauling his son out of the water.

Mari and Rhian rushed to help pull the soaking boy from the sea. He was slippery and heavy with the weight of the water, but in a second he was in the boat with them.

'Help!' Griff was still in the sea, struggling to stay above the waves with his shattered leg.

Rhian manoeuvred the boat towards him, and together they all managed to lift him in. He cried out in pain as his leg was dragged over the side, but he didn't thank anyone for rescuing him. He only had eyes for the creatures in the air above them. It was the dragons, whirling and folding and swirling in the sky like a flock of starlings.

Griff rooted awkwardly around in his pocket to pull out his phone, desperately trying to get his camera to work. But the waterlogged machine was useless. He threw it into the sea with a cry of frustration.

The dragons were beginning to turn away, flying out to sea. Only Gweeb was hanging back.

Mari and Dylan looked up at their little winged friend. With a final mischievous nod of her head, Gweeb banked and swooped and soared away with the others. Mari smiled. A broad, proud, loving smile. And a tear too. A happy tear.

'Please,' begged Griff. 'Follow them!'

He shook Rhian by the shoulders. 'FOLLOW THEM!' he roared.

Rhian just stared back, implacable. 'We're going home,' she told him.

Gareth gunned the engine, and the boat swung round, speeding towards the safety of the shore. Mari and Dylan and Griff all gazed back up into the sky to watch as the little flock of dragons disappeared out over the open sea.

'Hey now,' said Gareth, peering at the drenched figure huddled in the front of the boat. 'Aren't you that bloke off the TV?'

Griff dropped his head into his hands and began to weep.

Epilogue

The sun was setting majestically over the sea as a battered Land Rover pulled up in the car park next to the beach.

'So,' said Rhian as she and Mari climbed out, 'where's the best place to find fossils then?'

They started strolling towards the water's edge.

'Maybe this time I'll just look at the sunset,' said Mari.

Rhian put her arm round her. 'You won't stop doing what you love, will you, Mari?' she said. 'Because of what your dad did?'

Mari squeezed her mother's hand. They watched the waves crash against the shore as they had done for millions of years.

'I'm sorry I didn't tell you . . .'

'I just wanted him to be proud of me, Mum.'

'I know, Mari. I just wanted you to be proud of me too.' Rhian stopped and turned to face her. 'Maybe we should just be proud of ourselves. What do you think?'

Mari smiled, and buried her face in her mother's knitted jumper. It felt soft and warm. It felt of home.

'The world is waiting for you to be you,' said Rhian. 'Whenever you're ready. I won't hold you back.'

'You weren't, Mum, really you weren't,' whispered Mari. She looked up at her mother. 'Maybe I'll stick around here for a bit longer though. If that's OK . . .'

'Well, yes,' said Rhian with a wry smile. 'Especially now you're so good with animals.'

Mari punched her mum playfully on the arm. 'Well, I learned a bit about one animal,' she said.

'Though the main thing I found out, if I'm honest, is that she was better off by herself.'

Rhian shook her head. 'I don't believe that for a second, *cariad*.'

Mari was staring out at the orange sun slipping beneath the horizon when she noticed something odd. A dark speck in the middle of the sun. The speck became a dot, and the dot became a tiny silhouette. A flitting shape was coming towards them.

Rhian turned to follow Mari's gaze. The shape was getting closer, and now Mari could see it had wings, and an undulating body with a long tail following after. And then Mari could see that it was red, a bright ruby red, with a crest reflecting rainbows in the dying rays of the sun. At the last moment Mari saw two points of sparkling emerald before Gweeb careered into her chest.

'Gweeb!' she exclaimed. Gweeb raised her tail and spiralled it around Mari's finger. 'What are you doing here? Are you hurt? Has something happened to the others?'

Rhian looked closely at Gweeb. 'I can't see anything wrong with her.'

'Then why has she come back?' asked Mari.

'Maybe she's decided she's better off here,' said Rhian. 'With you.'

Mari looked back at the little dragon, hardly daring to believe that it might be true. Gweeb lifted her head, opened her mouth and, by way of approval, sent forth a little jet of flame.

'Ha!' said Mari delightedly. 'How are you doing that, now?' she asked, peering into Gweeb's jaws to get a closer look.

'Maybe she's just growing up,' said Rhian.

Mari smiled, and raised Gweeb up so that their eyes were fixed on one another. 'In that case,' she whispered very softly to the dragon, 'welcome home.'

Acknowledgements

The Secret Dragon is a book that is very close to my heart, because it is set in a place much like the one my parents live in, on the coast of South Wales. I've walked the cliffs and the beaches there, just like Mari does, for over twenty years, and though I've never really lived there myself, it has always felt like home. So as these are the acknowledgements, I have to acknowledge just how much I've been inspired by the Heritage Coast of the Vale of Glamorgan, and thank my parents – John and Lynda Clarke – for their love and support. I hope that

the people of the Vale will take Gweeb to their hearts, just as I have the beautiful place where they live. And I'd also like to thank my Welsh friends whose names I have slightly borrowed for a lot of the characters (you know who you are), and Reg Noyes for a little local lingo!

There are, however, two people without whom this book would not exist at all. Firstly, my editor, Ben Horslen at Puffin, who had always been on the lookout for a book about a dragon, but had never really expected it to be so little! Ben's faith in the story, trust in me, and excellent guidance throughout have literally made it all possible. Thanks too go to the incomparable Claire Wilson and her assistant Miriam Tobin at Rogers, Coleridge and White. Claire always knew the right home for this story, always gives the best advice and glides effortlessly like an agent swan, never revealing how hard she must be paddling beneath.

Thanks also to my fabulous cover illustrator, Ben Mantle and the interior artist, Simone Krüger, for bringing *The Secret Dragon* to life with such vibrancy and character; to Emily Smyth for creating the book's

wonderful look and feel; to Shreeta Shah and Sophie Nelson for making sure it all made sense; and to the whole team at Puffin for supporting Mari, Gweeb and me out in the big wide world. It really is an honour to have my name on such a beautiful book, and to be published by a company whose stories lined my own shelves as a child. And now my book will sit on the shelves of my own two daughters – Miriam and Rose – which warms my heart more than anyone will ever know.

Most importantly, I'd like to thank my sometime copy-editor, frequent sounding board, and always wife, Rachel. She has enabled me in so many ways to take the time I need to write and promote my books, and without her constant encouragement since I first put pen to paper, you would not be reading this.

And lastly, I'd like to dedicate this book to the memory of my great friend Nick Greenfield. He was endlessly curious about the world, and thought the best of everyone in it. There is something of his boundless energy in Gweeb, of his sheer zest for life, and that has been a huge inspiration to me. And I hope there is something of his spirit in this book that will inspire others too.

About the Author

When Ed Clarke isn't writing for kids, he is a film and television executive and producer, working with writers to make drama for grown-ups. He lives in North London with his wife and two young daughters, who would both desperately like a pet. He realizes they may be disappointed now if they get a rabbit rather than a dragon.

Dr Griff's
THE
DINOSAUR HUNTER

10

Fascinating
Fossil Facts!

1. In 2014 a new species of dinosaur was found on the coast of South Wales by Nick and Rob Hanigan. They called it the *Dracoraptor hanigani* – the 'dragon robber'. It was a distant relative of the T-Rex, but only two metres long.

2. A very common fossil that you can find on a beach is called a 'devil's toenail'! It is actually the fossilized remains of an extinct kind of oyster. (Its real name is *Gryphaea*.)

3. Mary Anning was twelve when she and her brother found the first correctly identified specimen of what came to be known as an *Icthyosaurus* or 'fish lizard'. However, we now know it wasn't actually a fish or a lizard, but a marine reptile.

4. Mary was also the first person to find a complete fossilized skeleton of a *Plesiosaurus* – the 'sea dragon' – but it was so strange-looking that at the time it was thought to be a fake.

5. You can still see the actual fossils that Mary Anning found back in the 1800s. They are kept at the Natural History Museum in London. And you can learn all about her at the Mary Anning Wing of the Lyme Regis Museum, which is built on the site of her former home and fossil shop.

6. Perhaps less well known is that Mary Anning was also one of the first people to identify fossilized dinosaur poo (called *coprolites*)!

7. Coelacanths – the fish known as 'living fossils', discovered by, and named after, Marjorie Courtenay-Latimer – can live for up to 100 years.

8. Even though they didn't discover them, a number of famous people have had fossilized species named after them, including Sir David Attenborough, Lady Gaga, and Mick Jagger from the Rolling Stones.

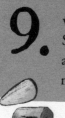

9. The largest dinosaurs to walk the earth were the Titanosaurs – a type of Sauropod – which grew to between 30 and 40 metres long, and weighed as much as ten African elephants.

10. The smallest dinosaurs were about the size of pigeons. The *Anchiornis huxleyi* weighed around 100 grams and was just over 30 centimetres long. It had feathers, scales and four wings!

Mari and Gweeb's adventures continue in

THE ORDER OF THE DRAGON

Coming in 2020